TALES
OF
BROKENNESS

TALES
OF
BROKENNESS

DON NORI

Destiny Image® Publishers, Inc.
P.O. Box 310
Shippensburg, PA 17257-0310

"We Publish the Prophets"

ISBN 0-7684-2074-1
(Previously published as *The Power of Brokenness*
ISBN 1-56043-178-4)

For Worldwide Distribution
Printed in the U.S.A.

This book and all other Destiny Image, Revival Press, MercyPlace, Fresh Bread, Destiny Image Fiction, and Treasure House books are available at Christian bookstores and distributors worldwide.

For a U.S. bookstore nearest you, call **1-800-722-6774**.
For more information on foreign distributors, call **717-532-3040**.
Or reach us on the Internet:
www.destinyimage.com

CONTENTS

PRELUDE

Brokenness is not for the faint of heart
or for those who weary easily, for she sees
weakness and storm, sorrow and pain.

BROKENNESS—the disdain of tyrants and the wonder of kings. Her mystery has eluded the intellectual and empowered the noble of heart. From her bosom flow the power and compassion to change the world, but she is as rigid and unforgiving as she is genteel and hopeful. Her wisdom instructs the hungry of heart, but her law defies the most persistent of religious antics. She is as stubborn as she is giving, demanding as she is predictable, and essential as she is eternal. She is born in the womb of divine passion and gives birth to reckless abandonment to His will.

Brokenness gives first, heals first, repents first, hopes first, loves first. She intercedes instead of accuses, covers instead of reveals, gathers and does not scatter, builds and does not destroy.

Brokenness promotes others, but she, herself, hides from the notoriety and clamor of the public eye. She does not parade her riches and her intimacy before the world, who will only use her secretly and discard her when the cost of embracing her is truly understood. She reserves herself for God alone. Her intimate mysteries are for His eyes and His heart only.

Brokenness is content with God's love and assurance. She does not covet the adulation of mere mortal man; neither does she demand attention or recognition, as though her gifts are only costume jewelry purchased in the marketplace of religious popularity and emotional fanfare.

No, Brokenness is not for the faint of heart or for those who weary easily. To find her requires a deliberate and personal decision—a resolve, as it were, to welcome a companion who comforts, consoles, and lights the way through the darkest of nights, but who also requires your very soul, reputation, pride, and glory. She is a companion in hiding, knowing, and understanding the frailty of the human species apart from God. She sees weakness and storm, sorrow and pain, even sin and personal iniquity. Still, rather than merely possessing the power to change and deliver, Brokenness is overwhelmed at a God whose love is so great, whose purpose so paramount, that He plunges us into His plan, saying so softly, so confidently, "Tend My sheep." Though you may argue, "Lord You don't know...," a reassuring smile breaks across His face and fills your soul with light. "Feed My sheep."

Brokenness knows her power. She understands that everything trying to separate and destroy will be done away with. So she accompanies those who walk on with a bruised hip. Confounded at His love, deeply grateful for His mercy, still struggling with sin, these determined believers tend His sheep. Brokenness never lets them forget their need of mercy, never lets them forget the grace that flows on their behalf.

Brokenness ministers from her knees. She carries a towel over her arm and a basin of water in her hands. She is content. She has found her niche, her resting place in the bosom of His heart. She serves her Lord with gentle admiration and yielding obedience. Though He may lead her into the darkest valley, down the loneliest road, or through a most confusing maze, Brokenness goes forward with quiet anticipation, knowing and accepting the path He has chosen. Her voice does not raise protest, neither does she devise an alternate prayer. She simply obeys. Her prayers are fervent as she prays with the sound of His heart beating in her spirit. Brokenness knows God's heart and plans. She can almost second-guess Him. Before He even says a word, Brokenness is ready, on her knees with pail in hand, waiting to do the Master's bidding.

Thus is the picture of Brokenness described in this book. Some will dismiss her as an intellectual fantasy. Others will regard her as being incomprehensible with the mind and untouchable with the heart. Still others will welcome her, savoring the fire she ignites in the spirit, and the hope and assurance she gives to the soul. To these, this book is written. To these, my prayers go forth. With these I share my confidence that a Church will emerge in this generation that has learned the power of Brokenness.

PROLOGUE

*I have heard her in the quiet
of my private place of prayer.*

BROKENNESS is calling to humankind. She has called to me many times. I have heard her in the quiet of my private place of prayer, as well as in the clamor of an all-too-busy lifestyle. I have heard her in the heat of an argument and in the gentleness of holding one of my children. Sometimes I have run quickly, desperately, to her side and have enjoyed the blessings of her friendship. Other times, I am ashamed to admit, I have been most reluctant to receive her counsel and to believe the truth she unveils from deep in my heart. Always she has been a faithful friend—refreshing and enlarging my understanding of who she is and who I am, encouraging me to go on when I think I can bear no more, bringing me to my knees when she shows me yet again where I must allow her to touch my pain and the hardness of my heart. She quietly waits through my stubbornness, knowing that the Lord will soften me so I can hear her counsel. She patiently endures my abuse when I grow tired of her tenacious pursuit. She is always there to reassure me that the rewards of cultivating her friendship are definitely worth it, for nothing can compare with the security of living with Brokenness in the very presence of Almighty God.

Now Brokenness calls to you as well. You cannot miss her cry for attention, but you can miss her gentle wisdom and the softness of her confession. Few realize that she possesses secrets that are worth more than the most priceless of pearls—secrets that will change you forever, that will open the windows of God's mercy and healing power.

Only those who trust Brokenness enough to draw her close benefit from her nearness. They discover that her wisdom and insight into their lives is far greater than the pain she inevitably brings with her. These folks are destined to discover her for themselves.

Don Nori
January 1997

Chapter 1

TREASURES IN EARTHEN VESSELS

I was carefully woven,
created for union from the beginning.

BROKENNESS. Before the heavens were set in place, before the earth was formed, Brokenness was birthed in the bosom of her Lord. She is the delight of His heart, the one in whom He finds His greatest pleasure. She knows His heart and sees all His plans. His intentions and purposes are not hidden from her eyes. Before He speaks she anticipates His words; His thoughts are open before her. Nothing escapes her watchful eye. She is always ready to do His bidding. Her faithfulness defies explanation. Beyond her passion to decrease that He may increase, there is little that moves her, little that excites her, and very little else that fulfills her.

When the world was first formed, Brokenness shared God's pleasure as light emerged from darkness and life from emptiness. With each new day, her anticipation grew to see what God would yet create. The delight in His eyes was reflected in hers as the words of His mouth brought forth dry land from the seas, plants and trees from the earth, and flying creatures to fill the skies. All held her admiring gaze as the beauty of creation unfolded.

Day after day, Brokenness beheld this creative power. She stood nearby as God, at the end of the day, surveyed all He had made. Each day she heard His satisfied declaration, "It is good."

As morning dawned on the sixth day, Brokenness watched intently as God formed the most splendid of all His creations. Brokenness did not understand at first, but this one was special indeed. She had watched as God had spoken the rest of His desires into time and space by merely the words of His mouth. This one He formed with His own hands, kneeling lovingly as He meticulously formed the man after His own heart. This new creation was splendid indeed, but not splendid, to be sure, for his speed, *since* many there are of God's creatures who are far more swift of foot; nor splendid for strength, *since* there are creatures of God's world who possess strength far beyond the capabilities of humanity; nor splendid for beauty, *since* beauty flows throughout all God's creation with indescribable magnificence and simplicity.

Nonetheless, Brokenness was drawn ever closer to this Creator God as He worked quietly and intensely over this simple lump of earth—a lump of earth that a few days ago, itself, did not exist. What was it about this man that commanded such consuming attention from the Lord? For as this clay began to take shape, the Lord's countenance grew brighter and brighter and a smile of utter satisfaction broke across His face. The light of His glory seemed to penetrate the form that lay before Him as He, oh so carefully, leaned back to observe His newest creation. Then, as a mother gently leans over her newborn child to give her a kiss, the Lord leaned over this new creation, and with all He had thus created watching intently, breathed into man the breath of His very own life.

Quickly God leaned back, still kneeling beside the man, to watch what would happen next. Brokenness moved closer. It was as if all creation paused with anticipation, waiting for the man to take his first breath. *What is this remarkable event I am watching?* Brokenness mused as her thoughts continued to search out an answer. *He is not an angel, yet he holds within him God's glory. He is but dust of the earth, yet the Creator is consumed with him more than with all else He has created.*

There was no time now for more speculation. All of her Lord's glorious creation waited to see this marvel unfold. The man just lay there for the longest time. He seemed to be glowing with an almost resplendent glory. Finally there were a few gasps, a slight cough, and the man began to breathe rhythmically and deeply, just as he had been created to do. Almost immediately, the man's eyes flittered open, blinked a few times to focus, and gazed upon Him who had just given him life. The man's lips began to quiver as he attempted speech for the first time. "My Father! My Father!" The man arose to embrace the Lord as humanity's first tear, a tear of joy, found its way down the man's face.

It was then that Brokenness came to understand both why another creature would not do and why she was privileged to be part of such an intimate and glorious creation. She saw that man had been especially designed to experience union with God Himself. He was created uniquely incomplete, as it were, for his destiny was dependent upon his dependency. This design of dependency was not from a morbid compulsion for control, but from God's eternal longing for union, for partnership.

Man was to be the throne upon which the Lord would sit and from which He would rule and reign in the earth. The whole world would see God's glory as it effervesced from the heart and life of these mortal men. "Marvelous!" Brokenness shook her head in wonder. "Mere flesh and blood will shine with the glory of the Creator God Himself! Yes, this species is splendid indeed—more than splendid, in fact," Brokenness celebrated. "This species is blessed above all others on the earth or under the earth, in the seas or in the air. Mankind is truly a wonder in the earth!"

As Brokenness watched the man embrace his Creator Father, she also came to understand the gravity of her own existence and exactly what it was that the Father expected. As that thought gripped her heart, the Father turned slightly so that His eyes would catch her gaze. *He knows, she thought to herself. He knows that I am finally understanding.*

Brokenness walked slowly to her Lord's side. "You have begotten me to serve You, and serve You I will." Then, as the Lord smiled, she turned and walked away.

Brokenness was consumed with thought. She pondered what the millennia would bring as she befriended each generation of humanity. *Will they listen to me? Will they understand the importance of my friendship? Will they welcome me as the companion the Father intends me to be? Or will they merely consider me an intrusion upon their plans, a stumbling block to their dreams and aspirations, and a thorn that intrudes upon their comfort?*

Suddenly Brokenness realized that the Lord was standing in front of her. Startled by His abrupt appearance, she embraced Him and wept on His shoulder. He spoke softly. "Their greatest asset is also their greatest liability." He paused for a moment, giving Brokenness time to understand His words. "Yes, I know how powerful they will feel as they exercise their option to choose their own destiny, but the power to choose is the very glory of My relationship with them. They must choose to serve Me. They must choose to love Me. Without this risk, without this choice, there can never be true love, true union, or true devotion to anything. But you, My dear, dear Brokenness, will be their secret weapon. You will be their hope. For only you can convince them to come to Me. Only you can convince them to relinquish their will to Mine and their dreams to My dreams. You alone can convince them to trust Me implicitly. You will show them mercy and bring them conviction, hope, repentance, and deliverance."

Strengthened by His words and the gentleness of His love, Brokenness again reaffirmed her devotion to her Lord and His creation, no matter what it meant she had to do. Bond servants are like that. Man would find that out, for Brokenness was God's plan for leading man into the willingness to accept the Lord's rightful place in his heart. The union Brokenness would one day create between man and his God would be a most formidable sight to their enemies. It would bring into being God's very plan for this struggling planet. Brokenness would be the catalyst, the means, the method of bringing the man and his Creator to a place of union and fellowship. *After all*, she reasoned to herself, *that is why God made the man. He has always wanted union and covenant.*

As the sixth day ended, the Creator God stood high on a mountain. His eyes rested lovingly on His newest creation, now sleeping comfortably, curled in a grass thicket in the valley below. Then He rocked the universe with the affirmation, "It is very good!"

Day after day God walked with these first human beings in the garden home He had prepared for them. He shared His hopes and dreams for them and for the world He had entrusted to their care. Time and time again He imparted new understanding, calling forth new skills to help them meet the demands of their responsibilities. Brokenness, a silent partner in these trysts, soon recognized that God had given the man and the woman everything they needed to fulfill God's dream for the earth. No gift, no ability, no talent was absent. Their destiny was within their reach. In fact, Brokenness took great delight in seeing how perfectly God had patterned them to fulfill His intentions. She saw how He had designed them to prosper, to flourish, and to win.

Yes, God had created these human creatures to work best when they cooperated with Him, when they understood His plans and purposes, when they obeyed His voice. It was as though they were gloves into which God fit His hand to accomplish His purposes in the earth. They needed Him to achieve maximum success. Brokenness delighted to see how implicitly the man and his companion trusted God's infinite wisdom and perfect knowledge to enlighten them and to help them to fulfill their responsibilities.

Thus they kept their daily trysts—the man, the woman, and their Father God. Love bound their hearts together and trust grew from their fellowship. Then came the evening when Brokenness sensed immediately that something was different, something was wrong. No joyful laughter or songs of praise wafted on the evening air. No eager footsteps or words of welcome greeted God and Brokenness. When they reached the gate, God turned slightly toward Brokenness and held up His hand. "I must go in alone this evening," He said gently.

No problem. I'll just wait here at the gate, Brokenness thought to herself, shuddering a little as God entered the garden alone.

"Adam, where are you?" God called.

At first there was no reply. Brokenness waited and wondered. Then a muffled voice called out, "I heard You walking in the garden and I was afraid, so I hid…"

The man, afraid? Brokenness thought. Why should the man be afraid? Have we not walked together many nights, now? What is there to be afraid of?

"…I was afraid because I am naked," the man said. "So I ran and hid when I heard the sound of Your voice."

"Who told you that you are naked?" the Lord asked with a sigh that said a thousand words.

Sorrow washed over Brokenness. She covered her face in grief, for she knew that the man had forfeited his place in paradise and had banished Brokenness from his life. There would be no more trysts in the garden in the cool of the day, no more warm embraces revealing hearts filled with love. The man had no room for them now.

"It was the woman," the man responded, "the woman God gave me as a helpmeet and companion! She gave me some fruit from the forbidden tree, and I took it and ate it."

"But that old snake tricked me!" the woman countered. "He tricked me into believing him."

Still in shock, Brokenness heard the words of the Lord. Pain resonated in His voice as though His heart was breaking. "Serpent, you are cursed for deceiving the woman. From now on you will crawl on your belly in the dust of the earth. The woman will hate you. She will finally strike you back."

The mist of evening settled over the garden as Brokenness heard the Lord speak to the woman, and finally to the man. His words pierced her very soul. Now they would know pain and suffering. Hardship and difficulty would hinder their path. No longer would they delight to hear the voice of their Father God. Neither would they enjoy His companionship, for they had no room in their hearts for His Spirit.

An angel with a fiery sword led them to the edge of the garden. Brokenness watched in disbelief as the man and the woman walked quietly through the gate. The clang of the gate behind them seemed to shake the night stillness like a bolt of lightning. Brokenness shuddered. Then she watched as the man and the woman disappeared into the darkness with their heads hanging low.

Brokenness wondered what would happen now to the relationship between God and the man He had so carefully formed with His own hands. It was clear by the compassion that flowed from the Father's heart that He would not abandon humanity. His heart was ever toward them. No, God would not forsake these most beloved of His creatures; He would not leave them desolate.

As the man and the woman left the garden, Brokenness followed them. She realized how difficult her task would now be. In pursuit of man's heart, she would have to go with him—to the very ends of the earth, if necessary. Such was the love of the Father, and such was His determination to bring the man into union with Himself.

Throughout the centuries since that fateful day, Brokenness has consistently and relentlessly courted humanity. Most have kept her at a distance. Some have acknowledged her presence. Fewer still have embraced her as friend.

Brokenness shares her testimony with these few, acknowledging the wisdom of King David, "The secret of the Lord is for those who fear Him. And He will make them know His covenant." Brokenness searches for those who sincerely fear the Lord. As soon as she sees a softening heart, she quickly arises to comfort and to give hope when there seems to be little or no hope. Those who are open to her wisdom enjoy her friendship and rely upon her healing balm—balm that flows from the very throne of God.

Brokenness watches for the softening of your heart, for even the slightest indication that you will welcome her intrusion. She has much she would like to share with you, but alas, you may be like the others who know of her by reputation alone. In your pain and confusion, you suspect that Brokenness holds only evil in her heart toward you; you doubt the purity of her motives and the accuracy of her discernment. And as you peer intently into the apparent hopelessness of your life, you wonder if her power is a little overrated. So you keep Brokenness far, far away.

Yet Brokenness, urged on by God's love and His undying commitment to your wholeness and well-being, continues to pursue you, to call you from afar. Time and time again she approaches you, looking for some indication of welcome, for even a small crack in the veneer with which you cover yourself.

Brokenness is near—as near as you will let her be. Her heart is completely toward you. She brings with her the life of God Himself. Yet she will not intrude upon your privacy. Contrary to your belief, she will only step forward when you allow her to approach you. Only then, when she perceives that you are ready to listen, ready to understand, ready to value what she has learned and experienced, will she attempt to touch your heart.

Yes, Brokenness most certainly will call you. She will beckon for you to come to her. At times she will absolutely pester you. She knows the value of her friendship to you. She understands that your destiny depends upon your life-long response to her. Though her cry for attention is piercing and persistent, her voice of testimony is soft and veiled. Only the very observant who have turned their hearts toward her, who desire her nearness, will hear the witness she bears. These humble ones will truly learn to understand and accept her courtship.

Chapter 2

THE COURTSHIP OF BROKENNESS

I am wooed by her love,
stricken by her devotion.

❧

BROKENNESS. One day you will meet her. Do not be surprised if she is nothing like what you have anticipated. She will not greet you as the gentle companion you will one day learn to appreciate. Neither will she approach you with a smile or an encouraging word. No, like a vain woman coveting the attention of everyone around her, Brokenness will accost you with a depth of reality you cannot ignore and a compelling voice that will demand a response.

Her insistent touch will constrain you to acknowledge her presence. She will want you to look into her piercing and unyielding eyes. She will touch the hip of your greatest strength and shatter it. She will find your most haunting weakness and burn its reality into your heart until it affects every relationship, colors every prayer, and carefully adjusts every attitude of your heart.

Brokenness confronts you and inhibits your steps as she relentlessly insists that you give her room in your life. Many have ruefully called her intimidating. Others have said she is unyielding and cold. "Ice runs through her veins. The woman has no mercy; she has steel for emotions," it has been said of her. Still others have complained, "She talks about mercy, but doesn't give in for a moment."

I fear we have all missed the point of mercy, for mercy's true nature is not the ability to give in, but the ability to see the end that is required and to do whatever is necessary to bring it about—even if what mercy must do appears to be unmerciful to the unbroken sense of reason. This is why man's first reaction upon seeing Brokenness is to look for a place to hide from her daunting gaze. For when she walks in, folks will pay any price to avoid her scrutiny. They scurry for rocks to hide under, masks to put on, and excuses to use. Anything that shields them from her penetrating insistence becomes a possibility.

As you will soon discover, Brokenness is not put off by your desperate attempts to run or hide. Should you peek out from your hiding place or risk a glance over your shoulder as you try to run away, you will meet her gaze. Brokenness knows what you are trying to do. There is absolutely no imagination to it. She has seen it again and again through-out the ages as frightened and frustrated folks have inadver-tently run from the very one who can lead them to the Mercy

Seat itself. Yes, Brokenness is very familiar with this response. But please understand. She has never gotten used to these desperate attempts to avoid her touch.

Brokenness must be content to stand in the shadows and wait for man to finally understand his need of her wisdom, her comfort, and her place of hiding. She follows and watches. Though she is quiet and keeps her distance, she analyzes your every move, waiting for your invitation. Should she happen to catch your eye, Brokenness leaps for your attention. With outstretched arms she reaches toward you, bidding you to receive her. Her haunting and persistent song calls you again and again, beckoning you to her side as though she knows something much deeper about you than even you have discovered. But when you turn away, she becomes silent again, watching, waiting, biding her time until she perceives that you are ready for her to try again to remove your masks, scale your walls, and penetrate your shields.

For a time you may be able to avoid Brokenness, or you may be successful in ignoring her insistent call. In truth, you may avoid a direct encounter with her for many days, weeks, or even years. Nonetheless, if God is truly merciful, which He is, and if you truly want your Lord's fullness in your life, which I hope you do, then without a single doubt, the time will come when Brokenness will find you no matter how you choose to hide. I suspect that sooner rather than later Brokenness will find you in a most vulnerable dilemma, giving her an opportunity to approach you.

If you are like many folks, deceptively believing that you are not in the danger that Brokenness knows you are in, you will not respond to her early on. "You are overreacting. This is not unto death. I can handle it," you insist to her.

"It is not within my nature to overreact," Brokenness responds gently. "You need my help. You need to repent."

Turning away from her in frustration, you continue on your way until another, more volatile situation comes along. Like the faithful companion she is sent to be, Brokenness draws near again. "Come hide in me," she entreats you. "Give me your pain that it may be turned into victory."

"I have no pain!" you again insist.

Brokenness walks quietly away. But take heart, she has not gone far. She knows that you will need her. Hopefully you will call upon her sooner rather than…well, rather than when you are facing a crisis that even she cannot over-rule. There are those situations that man gets himself into that cannot be resolved so easily as a simple confession or even a public repentance.

If you think Brokenness is tough at this point, as she gently tries to woo you into the loving arms of your Lord, wait until you are caught in a trap that requires her to come rushing to your aid in a desperate attempt to soothe the ensuing flurry of anger, tears, and remorse that your poor choices bring down upon you and your loved ones. This is the pain you will remember. This is the pain that will linger. This is the pain you most definitely want to avoid.

Wisdom dictates that you welcome Brokenness now. Though you fear what will happen, you must allow her to come near. Reluctantly you turn to her. At first Brokenness simply looks at you, scrutinizing every corner of your heart and mind. "Do not be afraid," she encourages you. "My work is not unto death, but unto the preservation of your life and the destiny your Lord has dreamed for you."

"It feels like it's unto death!" you grumble in response.

Brokenness smiles and rolls her eyes. "One day you will regret saying that to me."

"Don't count on it."

"Your unbrokenness is really evident today," is her quiet response.

Brokenness continues her silent but thorough scrutiny. If you look closely, you will discover something familiar about her—something warm, refreshing, even hopeful. You are about to think that you could get to liking her, when suddenly she breaks into your thoughts. "All right, this is going to hurt a bit, but…"

"Oh no it isn't," you blurt out, rather startled. "I didn't say that you could do anything to me."

Your interruption seems to surprise and disappoint Brokenness. As she backs away, you are again struck by the sense that you know this person better than you think you do. There is something so gentle about her that it warms your heart. "Where are you going?" you ask as she retreats.

"Not far," Brokenness responds quietly. "Not far."

Many days pass as Brokenness follows you everywhere you go. Desperately you try to go about your business, but her presence behind you haunts your every decision, your every temptation. You want to be angry with yourself for talking to her in the first place, for letting her poke around inside your heart as though you have some kind of infection. *What does she expect to find, anyway?* you think to yourself. *I'm a good person. I'm a strong believer. I love God! What does she think she could possibly find?*

"Do you want a list?" You jump with surprise and find yourself staring directly into her eyes—no, directly into her heart. "Do you want a list?" Brokenness repeats.

"I wasn't talking to you!" you quickly insist. Then more softly you ask, "Was I talking to you?"

"I thought you were."

"Well, I wasn't!"

"There's no one else around. Who were you talking to?"

"I wasn't talking to anyone. I was talking to myself."

"That's precisely right. You wouldn't dare try to justify the things you do in secret around real people. No one would believe the lies you are trying to tell yourself."

In utter exasperation you ask, "Who asked you to come here anyway?"

"Your Lord."

"My Lord? My Lord! Well, you can just tell Him…"

"Tell Him what?" Brokenness asks.

"You can just tell Him…thank you." With that statement, you take your first real step toward Brokenness. It is not easy, but I do not remember saying that it would be easy. Nevertheless it is essential, not just for the fulfillment of your destiny but for your life itself.

So as Brokenness continues her pursuit, fear grips your heart. You aren't ready for this. You don't want to face yourself or your sin. You have been hiding for so long. No one even sees you…yet. But your sin has bound you, and it still binds you. *Perhaps I can still find the strength to run from her*, you fantasize as you begin to realize how arduous are her demands and how exacting her requirements. But you know you cannot, and very deep inside you know that you do not want to run from Brokenness, you do not want her to give up on you. In spite of the outward struggle, in spite of the drive toward self-rule, you really do want Jesus to be Lord. Yes, deep in your heart, you want her to win, and win completely.

Trembling, you slowly turn to face Brokenness. As you look into her eyes, that sense of the familiar is there again, overwhelming you. Although she is still a foreboding figure, and her countenance is as stern as ever, there is something very different about her, something you did not notice as you tried to avoid her.

Brokenness holds your gaze. Slowly you remember where you've seen this look before. Tears stream from your eyes as you see your Lord's compassion and abiding love in the heart of Brokenness. Immediately she is beside you, holding you as you sob uncontrollably in her arms. "My Father! My Father!" is all you can say. His love floods your inner being as Brokenness celebrates her first victory in your life.

"You do not think a love so profound that it drove Him to the cross could be discouraged now, do you?" Brokenness comforts you. "His love can handle far more than you would expect." Such gentleness and love! Such concern for your well-being! You are overwhelmed by her compassion.

The pain is now nearly unbearable. You want to stay and embrace Brokenness, but the pain! Can you stand this pain that you had long ago buried and nearly forgotten?

Fear clutches at your heart. *You must run from her,* your thoughts scream at you. *You must run far from her. Surely you cannot ignore all this pain she has brought back!*

Still you long to experience the gentleness and compassion of Brokenness. *But I need her warm embrace.*

But what will this warmth cost you? Have you thought of that? You know that you cannot bear anything more than the pain that already crushes your heart.

Torn by the war within, you stand there undecided, pondering what you should do. Although you do genuinely want to welcome Brokenness into your life, you wonder what else she might require, what forbidden door she might attempt to open. Then you drop your gaze and slowly begin to back away, shaking your head and thinking, *The price of her friendship is too great.*

How relieved you are when Brokenness offers no resistance. It is as though she is willing to give you some distance now that you have finally faced her for the first time. For now she seems to be satisfied with the small crack in your heart of stone. Perhaps she knows that you are not ready to yield to her intense scrutiny and the change such scrutiny will require.

In any case, her eyes follow you as you turn and walk away. When you dare to glance back at her one last time, you are secretly glad to discover that she follows you more closely than she ever did before. Still, her resolute gaze fixed on you makes you shudder. Thus Brokenness always keeps you within the sound of her voice, within the inspection of her penetrating eyes.

Perhaps you forget about your silent companion as the pain she inflicted begins to fade. Maybe you hope that Brokenness will be satisfied to keep her distance now that you have finally faced her. Nevertheless, just when you think you have begun to recover from your first meeting with her, Brokenness again comes close to you. As her compelling voice speaks your name, you realize how foolish you have been to think that you could escape her demanding presence. Again the choice is yours: Will you turn to face her, or will you run?

Should you choose to face Brokenness, you may find her countenance just as foreboding as the last time you met, or you may discover that this encounter is not nearly so fearful as your last experience. But should you try to run, you will find that evading Brokenness is more difficult now that you have given her even a slight entrance into your heart.

"This is not the time to run. Do not waste this opportunity," Brokenness gently instructs you.

Still you are not willing to yield to her entreaty. Standing there with your arms crossed over your chest and your eyes cast down to the ground, you stubbornly act as though she has not spoken. *I may not be able to avoid this insistent pursuer,* you think, *but at least I don't have to look at her.*

How surprised you are when firm fingers lift your chin and force you to raise your head. Almost against your will you glance upward with flashing eyes that reveal the depth of your fear. "I believe we have already talked!" you mutter between clenched teeth.

"Yes, we have, but we still have much to talk about, much to heal!"

Resolutely you glance away, trying to hide the fear and anger that churn inside. Brokenness is not fooled. "You will thank me for this someday," she says.

"Is that all you can say?"

Your response is most unkind, but Brokenness understands your pain even better than you do, so she easily overlooks this private emotional outburst. She is not daunted by your anger. Neither does she give any sign of relenting, of giving you a way of escape. Guided by her knowledge that your resistance only makes it worse as you recoil from the sound of her voice and cower beneath her gaze, Brokenness tries yet again to persuade you to accept this meeting.

When you glance quickly in her direction, her eyes meet yours. For long moments she holds your gaze. She cannot force you to welcome her, but she will not give up easily. She exhibits no hesitation or insecurity. The shifting glances that reveal your desperation to escape are no surprise to her. Indeed, she is no stranger to all the wiles of men who seek to avoid her scrutiny.

Brokenness remains alert lest you try to deceive her or to evade this moment of decision. She watches carefully to see what you will do next.

Your fear mounts as it becomes increasingly evident that Brokenness will not budge. Though you search frantically for an escape, you know in your heart that you cannot evade her. Indeed, you are not sure you even want to. Truly you know that you have no choice. You are a bond slave of the Lord. You must decrease and He must increase—but at what cost?

Finally you relent, collapsing into her waiting arms as the fight drains out of you. Tears stream down your face, and sorrow and pain once again fill every fiber of your being. Although you still want to resist, to remove yourself from her arms, Brokenness holds you close. She knows that change will begin deep in your heart if you only will surrender.

In that moment you realize something that will have a profound impact on your future. Brokenness is not the messenger of satan you had assumed her to be. She is a friend sent by your truest Friend—your most merciful Lord. Now you realize that you must yield to her, that you must give yourself to her work in you.

Gradually a sweet sensation begins to soften your pain. You open your eyes to find that Brokenness, kneeling beside you, has pulled the blessed balm of Gilead from her satchel and is applying it to your need. Now a smile plays across your face as you accept the bittersweet quality of this experience. Yes, her touch has brought the pain you have so feared; but Brokenness has also brought comfort and a hope for wholeness that you had long ago abandoned.

You know in your very soul that you must feel her healing touch yet again. You are certain that you will meet her, even seek her, in the days ahead. Without another word, Brokenness confirms the many encounters that yet await you. You will indeed have many more opportunities to give yourself to her power and to respond to her wisdom.

Resting now in her arms and grateful for her presence, you are becoming more confident in her love. You have discovered the peace Brokenness brings when you stop fighting her touch and avoiding her presence. Yes, your next experience with her may be just as difficult, just as frightening, as this encounter. Her razor-sharp stare may seem to be just as cold. Nevertheless, the next time you meet Brokenness, you will recognize her for who she is—one who brings God's mercy and love. You will understand that she brings not only pain but comfort. She not only wields a piercing light that cuts to the very depths of your heart, demanding truth and humility, but she also carries with her a healing balm that comes lovingly from the hand of your gracious Lord.

Chapter 3

THE WISDOM OF BROKENNESS

I have confessed nothing to her,
yet she knows me better than I know myself.

BROKENNESS. Her voice echoes through the years of your life, bidding you to accept her presence—no, to covet her companionship. So persistent is her pursuit that you might think she is arrogant and even egotistical. So she might seem to be, since Brokenness is not easily discouraged. Her stubborn perseverance, born from loyalty to you and to her Lord, will not permit her to stop calling to you or to concede that you will never welcome her.

You are the one who decides your experience with Brokenness, by the distance you keep yourself from her. Although at first glance she appears to be cold and calculating, and her voice puts fear into your heart, you will find her to be quite different if you welcome her friendship and value her nearness. Those who have allowed Brokenness to come close to them testify that her demeanor changes dramatically when an intimacy occasioned by nearness begins.

Behind the stern resolve you encounter when you first meet her lies a gentle, entreating heart that captivates all who welcome and desire her presence. Even though her job is to help you see yourself honestly, she never intends to harm or embarrass you. Yet by her very nature she is not satisfied until you notice her greeting and invite her to draw near. Then you discover that her persistence in showing you who you really are brings the ultimate release and peace you have been seeking all your life.

Thus Brokenness pursues you day after day, crying out to you repeatedly until you finally acknowledge her— perhaps briefly at first, but then with more consistency and attention as you begin to regard her as your friend. Brokenness affirms the wisdom of knowing as well as admitting your limitations, of confessing and taking responsibility for your failures and your sin. This is truly the first step in experiencing genuine co-labor with the Lord. It is in this that you see how much you need Him to overcome sin, to receive strength and encouragement, and to do what you are called to do.

When you permit Brokenness to come near, she drops her voice to a whisper so only the two of you can hear her words of wisdom. For although she shouts to get your attention, Brokenness will not broadcast the intimate details of your life. Those who welcome her intimacy find that she is wonderfully compassionate and discreet. She is willing to work with you and for you as you discover your weaknesses and hidden sin. When a man will not deal directly with Brokenness in the personal, yet critical, issues of life, God sends others to expose these hidden hindrances to progress. These persons are usually far less tolerant and loving than Brokenness.

Hence these attributes of Brokenness become blessed qualities to the wise of heart and the humble of spirit. They are never so evident as when she begins to work in your heart to show you who you truly are. For you see, Brokenness is never concerned for herself. She knows who she is and what the Father expects of her, and she is content in His service. No, her burden is for you because she has discovered that you don't truly know yourself. Oh, you certainly have pictures and patterns by which you measure yourself, but Brokenness uncovers many of them for what they are—lies that have enslaved you for many years, keeping you from the Source who catapults you into your destiny.

So Brokenness begins by gently questioning your picture of yourself. "Why do you keep expecting to fail?" she asks. "Don't you understand that God is your heavenly Father and He formed you to be like Him and to share His abilities? You are not insignificant, as you judge yourself to be; neither were you made to stumble and fall. God created you to flourish, prosper, and succeed like He does. You only fail because you will not admit your need of God. He designed you to accomplish everything He planned for your life. You are His masterpiece, fashioned carefully and pre-cisely to do exactly what your destiny requires."

"Me, a masterpiece?" you interrupt incredulously. "You're trying to tell me that I am God's masterpiece, creat-ed precisely and intentionally to do whatever He wants? Some masterpiece I am! Why last week…"

Brokenness places a restraining finger on your lips, silencing the tirade that quickly reveals your tendency to put yourself down. She is not surprised by your outburst, for she knows how frequently you dwell on your mistakes and the smallness of who you think you are. Yet smallness is a mat-ter of perspective, and value is a judgment not of accom-plishment, but of possibilities. Smallness is of no effect when God enters a life. It smacks against the reality of His plan and His hunger to work with you and in you moment by moment. Brokenness has watched for years as you have doubted your value and underestimated your abilities, but she will not permit you to continue your destructive assess-ment. She understands the power of words, how easily you can become what you—and others—say you are.

For an instant you hesitate, wanting to walk away, yet sensing that something of infinite value is at stake. In that moment Brokenness quickly blocks your path, laying a restraining hand on your arm. When you do not move, she begins talking. "God knows what happened last week, but He also heard you weeping in repentance. What you do not realize is that He forgave you and dropped that sin into the sea of forgetfulness. Why do you continue to remind God of what He has already forgiven?" For this you have no answer, so Brokenness goes on. "Your problem is not what you think it is. It has nothing to do with how God made you, but with how you see yourself."

Brokenness pauses, deep in thought, then continues. "Let me share a secret with you. God doesn't expect you to make it alone. He created you to live empowered by His Spirit and driven by His love. He knows that you cannot be effective or successful on your own. He made your physical body and your soul to flourish and reach their maximum fulfillment when they are joined with Him. Your completeness comes only in union with His Spirit. Like a husband is not complete without his wife, you are not complete without the Spirit of God. You need the Holy Spirit, and the Holy Spirit needs you. Each can stand alone, but you and God's Spirit were meant to soar together, achieving your ultimate satisfaction and success as you flow in beautiful harmony.

"In truth, so careful was God in designing you, that He fitted you to Himself like a glove into which He slips His hand to accomplish His purposes," Brokenness explains, carefully taking note of the disbelief that is still reflected in your eyes. "You were created to perfectly fit His Spirit. Your humanity and God's Spirit are precisely paired. A glove without a hand is of little use; and a hand without a glove is limited and restrained in what it can do. So by yourself you cannot accomplish what God created you to do. You need His Spirit to fulfill your destiny."

You are silent when Brokenness stops speaking. This new picture of yourself is difficult to understand, let alone believe. In fact, you almost wonder if Brokenness knows what she is talking about. A quick glance at her convinces you that she believes this precious secret. Her eyes are clear and pure, her expression open and engaging. No mask hides her face. Her heart of love and compassion effervesces from her entire body.

"How can you be so certain?"

A smile lights the face of Brokenness and a faraway look enters her eyes. You have the impression that she is not really seeing you. It is as though she is looking past you, perhaps to another time or place. "I am certain," Brokenness whispers softly, so softly that you must lean closer to hear her words, "because I saw the Lord create the first man. How lovingly and carefully He formed that lump of clay into a human being—a creature filled with His own resplendent glory. All creation seemed to hold its breath as it watched God intently and meticulously work until He was satisfied. The smile on His face dazzled all who were there, but the crowning moment came when God knelt and breathed into this creature His own breath of life, and the man opened his eyes and recognized his Creator and Father. I will never forget his joyous first words, 'My Father! My Father!'

"Since that day, I have seen God breathe life into many people, each created to be like Him and to share in His marvelous Kingdom. Oh, they haven't looked the same on the outside, but I quickly learned that the surface of a person reveals little, if anything, about who he truly is. What matters is the person inside, the person who has within him the compassion and love to inspire, encourage, and yes, even heal. It is what God places within each person that matters. These gifts and abilities buried deep inside reveal the marvelous diversity that is in God Himself—abilities to dream and plan, to create and design, to prosper and succeed. These are the aspects of humans that show how precisely God created men and women to be like Him. Each is different, yet the same. Each shares the likeness of God, although their individual gifts and abilities suit them for differing tasks.

"I remember the Creator's delight as He knit you together in your mother's womb. No detail was missed as you were wonderfully made. He created you exactly the way you needed to be to give His Spirit a home and to do everything He purposed long before you were conceived. He reviewed your days carefully to be sure that each gift and personality trait was designed into you so that you could flourish, succeed, and prosper on this earth. The words of consecration He spoke over you while you were in the womb still resound in my heart. These words are no less significant than those spoken over the Old Testament prophet Jeremiah, whom the Lord consecrated and appointed as a prophet to the nations before he was even born!

"But alas, you do not understand who you are. Your picture of yourself is very different from how I see you—and how God sees you. Years of abuse, excuses, and inappropriate expectations have convinced you that you have no value, that you cannot succeed, that there is no reason even to try."

Brokenness looks at you. She understands your frustration. She feels your pain. Gently she squeezes your hand to draw you from your thoughts. "Dear child," Brokenness questions you, "why are you so discouraged when you fail? Why are you afraid to believe that you can be more? You have been trying to do by yourself what God intends for you to do with Him. Should it really surprise you that a part cannot accomplish as much as the whole? Your failure does not mean that God made a mistake when He formed you. No, your failure simply reveals that you need God's part—the indwelling presence and power of His Spirit in your heart—before you can begin to fulfill all He dreams for you.

"Yes, I know," Brokenness adds, laughing, "you are surprised that God has dreams for you. He has not forgotten them! Your inability to be who you think you should be has not changed how He sees you or what He has planned for you. Just like you dream for your family's future, God dreams for you. Exactly the way you make plans and work hard to help your dreams come true, God works to make His dreams come true.

"That's precisely why He sends me to you—to help His dreams come true. He knows that your heart cannot be a place where He can build His 'dream house' until you welcome me as your friend and intimate companion. Don't you see that I am part of His provision for you, a blessing from His hand to bring you into your destiny? You need

Brokenness in your life so that God's glory may flow through you freely to a despondent world.

"God's heart is toward you. You are never out of His thoughts. Always He is bringing you into circumstances, putting you with people, and leading you into situations that will refine your heart and prepare you for His glory. He longs to live with you, taking pleasure from being with you in a relationship of love, intimacy, and commitment. He wants you to know Him and to understand His heart and His thoughts toward you.

"But first you must allow me to have my way with you, since God's Spirit dwells with those who are humble and broken of heart. Only as I touch the eyes of your heart will you honestly be able to see both who you now are and who you can yet become. And only as you embrace me as your closest friend will you truly be able to hear my voice."

Chapter 4

THE CONFESSION OF BROKENNESS

I have found a mirror that does not
deceive, a looking glass that never fails.

❈❋❈

B ROKENNESS comes to you quietly, compassionately. To the comfort of your private place of prayer, where a man does real business with God, she comes. She hears your complaint before the Lord. She hears your struggle with sin—the sin in your heart, the sin you hate. She hears you pleading for mercy, if not for deliverance, from the things that so often seem to separate you from your Lord.

"You don't know what it's like!" you say. "This human body You gave me cannot succeed. Why did You make me like this? If You knew I was going to fall so often, why did You give me a nature that loves to sin? I just can't go on like this!"

"Do you feel better now?" Brokenness interrupts.

"What? What do you mean, 'Do you feel better?' I don't feel good at all!"

"I don't think it made Adam feel better either," Brokenness muses almost to herself. "It never makes you feel good when you blame someone else for your sin."

"Do you mind? I am trying to pray here. I am trying to…"

"You are trying to blame God for your sin," Brokenness interrupts. "It didn't work for Adam and it won't work for you."

Confused, but undaunted, you go on. "Well, I didn't make me like this. I can't help it if God made me this way."

"I know it will be a startling discovery," Brokenness begins, "but don't you think it is just the easy way out to blame God, your loving Creator, for everything that is wrong in your life? Do you actually believe that you sin and suffer the terrible woes you face because of the way God made you?

"It is the height of human arrogance to blame God for humanity's inability to keep themselves from sin. You have been blame-shifters from the beginning. Deep inside you are so convinced of your self-control and personal discipline. This is the only way to ultimately accept your uncontrollable drive toward sin. You must create a theology that blames your Lord for making you in such a way that you are set up for failure no matter how hard you try. What you must learn is that God created you as perfect as you can be apart from the Spirit of God who gives you life and the ability to fulfill your destiny. There is no manufacturer's flaw. You were not made defective."

"Why then do I feel defective? Why do I struggle so with sin?"

"Ah," Brokenness replies. "I've been waiting to share my second secret with you. This truth will not be easy to accept, but hear it you must if we are to be friends."

You are silent for a moment, pondering these words. You search the face of Brokenness for a clue, some indication that will prepare you for what is to follow. *Can this truth be that hard?* you wonder. *The first secret Brokenness shared was not so bad*, you reason.

Slowly you nod, indicating that you are ready to hear this second mystery of Brokenness. But you are not prepared for the solemn expression that comes into her eyes just before she speaks, nor for the piercing gaze that cuts to your very soul, reminding you of another day when you hid from her to avoid this scrutinizing stare.

Fear clutches at your heart in the instant before Brokenness speaks. Perhaps you are not ready, after all, for this confession—whatever it is. You drop your gaze, avoiding the probing eyes that study you.

Brokenness watches you for a moment longer as one emotion after another crosses your face. "You sin because you give evil a personal invitation to enter your life," she reveals. "Adam, using his own free will, invited sin into his life. So do you. Hence you, like Adam, need a savior and a deliverer."

Could you have heard Brokenness correctly? "I don't invite evil into my life," you counter with predictable stubbornness. "It's just always been there. Sin has been part of my life for as long as I can remember. It's not fair to hold me responsible for the condition of my life."

"That is just the point," Brokenness interrupts. "You are responsible for your life. You do invite evil into your heart."

"God made me with the capacity to sin," you protest.

"No!" Brokenness responds with more authority than you have ever sensed from her. "God made you with the capacity to choose. Yes, you must be taught how to make the right choices in life, but the responsibility for choosing is ultimately yours."

"My son did not need to be taught to steal a cookie just before dinner!" you respond quite confidently.

"Your son took a cookie the first time because he was hungry. He had to be taught not to do it. The second time he stole the cookie. It was his choice to disobey you after you had taught him the right response. That is where sin entered."

You want desperately to continue your protest, but Brokenness holds up a restraining hand, as though to stay your words. "You must also understand," Brokenness continues, "that sin is not part of you. It is an invader that comes into your life and corrupts the beautiful creature God made you to be. Since you have not allowed yourself to submit to the power of Christ within, sin rules your mortal body. You are made complete, yet incomplete; perfect, yet needy. You must work with another force to function in God's Kingdom.

"A lamp can be manufactured to perfection. Yet unless it is lit, it cannot fulfill the purpose for which it was made. All its intricate parts and carefully designed features cannot make it give light. Why? It was not made to function alone.

"A kite is designed and built to go to the heights of the atmosphere, but without the wind it lies powerless on the ground. It is earthbound despite its perfection. It was not made to fulfill its destiny alone.

"If you choose to cooperate with God, His Spirit lives the life of Christ through you. On the other hand, if you choose not to cooperate with Him, the life of sin and corruption is lived through your mortal body. Something will give you power. Something will move you on. You must choose what that will be."

Suddenly you hear a voice you recognize all too well. "You can't be serious!" leers this voice that resounds in your mind. "You don't really believe this nonsense, do you? Why, you're just plain bad. Look at all the awful things you have hidden in your heart. That's all part of you. It's who you are. Don't think you can avoid the real issue."

Brokenness quickly moves closer as the evil one looms over you, trying to convince you that you are worthless and far too sinful for even God to forgive. Gently she whispers for your ears alone, "This is not true. Do not believe these lies. God made you in His image to carry His glory. The sin that has invaded you is keeping you from your destiny."

When you fail to respond to her counsel, Brokenness becomes more insistent, trying to turn you toward her Lord. "Don't run away from me," she pleads. "I can help you through this if you will let me. I can't take away your sin, but I know that my Lord can help you. All you need to do is repent of the sin that is in your heart."

Brokenness watches the struggle that is evident on your face. She knows how hard it is for you to disarm the voices that have deceived you for years. So she tries again to help you understand.

"Sin is like a spy," Brokenness begins. "He can only do damage until you discover and disarm him. When he goes undiscovered, or should you refuse to acknowledge his presence, he is free to continue his beguiling work. But as soon as you acknowledge that he is there, lurking in a place where he has no right to be, he loses his power. He can no longer hurt you once he is disarmed.

"Sin works in the same way. It is no more a part of you than a spy is part of the country he infiltrates. Nevertheless, until you recognize and confess the sinful attitudes, thoughts, and actions that consume your heart, you give the evil one license to do whatever he wills."

Brokenness, seeing the growing yearning in your heart for freedom and wholeness, questions you quietly: "What do you do when your body is seriously ill?"

"I go to the doctor, of course."

"Then do the same for your soul. Go to the Great Physician, the only One who can heal you."

Startled, you turn to look at Brokenness. "Go to the Great Physician?"

"Yes," Brokenness answers. "When your body is ill, you go to the doctor and freely tell him your story. 'There is something wrong with me. I need you to help me. I am afraid that something has gotten into me that is not part of me and does not belong in me. I'm tired of feeling this way. I can't go on like this or it will kill me. Find out what is wrong and do whatever is necessary to get rid of this disease. Operate, if you have to. Give me drugs or radiation. Do whatever you must do to make me well. I want to be rid of whatever is taking away my physical health. I am willing to alter my lifestyle, lose a limb, or make a change in priorities. I want this thing out of me! I want to live!' This same life-and-death attitude toward your soul is essential if you want your heart to be cleansed and made whole."

"Repentance?" you ask weakly.

"Yes," Brokenness affirms, "classic repentance—but don't forget that you are not repenting of something that is part of your humanity. The sin in your heart is an invader that corrupts you. There is no need to shelter it. When you banish it from your life, you are not exiling part of yourself. So let go of it. Repent as often as you need to until your heart is cleansed and whole. I'll be right here to help you. Just lean on me when you are having a hard time seeing the truth of sin's invasion. Talk to your Lord as you talk to a doctor, 'Lord, sin has invaded my body. I don't like it, I don't want it, but I keep doing it. It is taking control of me and starting to separate me from You. I need Your help to get rid of it. It is not mine. I am on Your side. Please forgive me and deliver me from its power.' "

"But...but...you don't..." you begin to protest.

"Do not resist this gentle nudge from your heavenly Father. Just start now to allow God to show you where sin has taken root in your life. You will never be free of sin's influence until you give the Lord free reign to work in your heart. In fact, you will hold on to what you are, broken and battered as you may be, until you truly see the extent of the mess this invasion of sin has made in you, and you confess your loathing for sin's infestation without excuse, without compromise, and ultimately, without hesitation."

Now Brokenness is quiet. She takes a few steps back until she is standing a short distance from you. There is so much more she would like to say to you, but you have heard enough. You must first determine how you will respond to what you have already heard. For long moments she watches you as you go back into prayer. Then she reluctantly turns and walks away.

Brokenness returns to her home close to the heart of God the Father. She looks forward to the day when you allow her to stay with you while you uncover yourself before the Lord, admitting to Him the sin and pain you have hidden deep inside. Yet she will not force you to accept her presence or the truths she brings to your heart. You must receive them willingly.

For now it is enough that you are taking another important step in your pilgrimage through life. You are learning to obey, even when it hurts...a lot. Yes, Brokenness understands how hard it is for you to seek God's mercy and forgiveness and to admit your need of Him. She is no stranger to the pain that comes to all who begin to respond to her. The cry of her heart is simply that you will learn to separate the essence of your being from the sickness that has invaded your soul. Then and only then will you come to value and seek her abiding presence.

Brokenness dares to believe that one day you will understand and value her whispered confession. Thus she waits and watches, looking for the next opportunity when you will welcome her approach, when you will truly come to understand the value of her influence.

Chapter 5

The Influence of Brokenness

She is behind me. She is beside me.
She is in front of me.

B ROKENNESS is quiet as she watches from a distance. She has shown you her wisdom and made her confession. She will approach you no more until she sees what you do with her secrets. It is enough that you have heard these truths: you are God's creation, created carefully and precisely to live in union with Him; sin is an invader in your humanity, albeit an invader you welcome by your personal invitation. Now Brokenness must simply wait.

At first you are relieved that Brokenness has distanced herself from you. You are much more comfortable when she is not near. Yet her words replay themselves in your mind, begging for an audience, for a chance to be taken out and reviewed.

Back in your private place of prayer, you begin to defend yourself. *God, this is so unbelievable. Can You truly use me? I mean, who would think that You designed me to work intimately with You? No way! I'm nothing like You. I mean, You are so holy, and I am…well, so sinful. How can Brokenness say that You made me to work with You in harmony?*

And this invader business. Is it really possible that I invite sin into my life? I certainly wouldn't think so. It seems like I'm always trying to get away from it. Sure, I don't have much success, but I am trying, God. Even when I confess my problems and ask You for help, I still end up right where I don't want to be!

Brokenness, from afar, observes the confusion and frustration etched in your face. She hears your perplexed sighs and yearns to help you, but she will not intrude. She knows that she cannot force you to receive her. Difficult as it may be, she will not prevent you from casting aside her pearls, rejecting them as too unbelievable and certainly far too difficult to live out. So she waits and watches, eagerly looking for an opportunity, an invitation, to approach you yet again.

For a time the confusion in your heart and mind consumes your attention. On the one hand, you instinctively know that Brokenness is telling the truth. You know that you will not be happy until you believe her secrets and accept the changes they will most assuredly bring. On the other hand, you shrink from the pain of accepting her wisdom as your wisdom and her confession as your own. The memory of her compelling voice warns you to have nothing more to do with her. Yet...

Almost against your will, you glance over your shoulder to see where Brokenness is and what she is doing. *Will her nearness always be so difficult? you wonder. Can I possibly come to accept, and even enjoy, her presence?*

Brokenness, feeling your gaze, looks up and meets your eyes. You look at each other, each measuring the other's expression. For a time neither one moves. Then slowly Brokenness begins to speak, almost as if she is requesting your permission to go on. You nod and she comes closer.

"Would it help you," Brokenness asks quietly when she is near enough for you to hear her, "if you could see how my influence has changed someone else's life?"

"That might be a good idea," you respond slowly.

"Come then," Brokenness invites. "Let's see how my friendship with the one who walked on the water made a difference in his life."

"Peter!? The apostle Peter? I can never be like him. Can't you choose an ordinary person?"

"Oh, Peter was quite ordinary," Brokenness replies. "Perhaps you've never noticed that, or maybe his friendship with me is what made him appear to be something other than ordinary. Come, let me show you how my influence changed Peter's life."

Skeptically, you agree. *How can this possibly help me? you think. I'm nothing like Peter.*

"I'm sure you remember Peter's story," Brokenness begins. "Throughout his life he failed again and again. His impulsive outbursts were a source of embarrassment for all the disciples and, I dare say, a source of slight exasperation even for the Lord. But the night of his last supper with Jesus became his most difficult experience.

"How upset Peter was when Jesus predicted that he would deny Him. I cringed as I heard Peter promise to die with Jesus, if that's what it took.

"As you know, Peter fulfilled Jesus' prediction. I caught up with him as he ran out into the night and cried with all his heart. Before Peter denied Jesus, I had courted him from afar. That night, when I held him as he cried, we became much better acquainted.

"When a man sees himself for the first time—I mean, really sees himself—he gets to know me very well. Peter could accept neither what he had done nor the new picture of himself he had seen. Before Jesus' death, he had been a leader in the band of disciples, part of the inner circle. Now he wasn't sure he should be part of the group at all. It wasn't pleasant being with Peter that night as I tried to redirect his sorrow to resolve, his pain to determination, his hardness to mercy, and his fear into love. He had a hard time learning that pain is not a bad thing—perhaps because he was very high on himself, and the higher you are…well, let me continue.

"I couldn't believe what I was doing two days later when Peter made a desperate attempt to run from himself, and I chased the Lord's chosen down a dirt path to the sea. Even though Peter had allowed me to come nearer that awful night when he denied Jesus, he certainly didn't consider me an intimate confidante—at least not yet. So I followed him at a distance. I expected that he would need me the next morning when he saw his Lord. When Jesus greeted him from the beach, I knew that I was at the right place.

"Peter was still in the boat when he recognized his Friend. It didn't take long for him to jump into the sea and swim ashore. He burst out of the water and fell at Jesus' feet. Our Lord gently took his arms and helped him to stand. Peter hung his head as Jesus began to speak.

" 'Peter, do you love Me?'

"In that moment I stepped close to Peter as he faced his Lord," Brokenness continued. "I knew Peter was trapped by his sinfulness and the weakness of his humanity. Now Jesus had found him fishing. He knew that Peter had simply run away.

I wonder if He knows? Peter thought. *Does He know how my boasting arrogance failed Him?*

"Jesus just waited for Peter to speak. I knew that his heart was breaking. I also saw that my Lord was gently bringing Peter to the end of himself. So I stepped even closer to

Peter. He needed me as he faced his humanity and his sin. It was after I touched him, when he felt my arm around him, that he found the courage to tell the Lord that his love was not as deep as he had claimed.

" 'Tend My lambs,' Jesus responded. Peter was stunned. He stood in total silence, which was rather unusual for Peter. The Lord moved closer to Peter and whispered to him, 'Peter, do you love Me?'

"Peter nearly collapsed into my arms as all his fears and uncertainties came pouring out. 'Oh, Lord, You don't understand. I'm not going to give my life for You. I don't love You that much! You're not hearing me. All this time I told You that I had this undying love for You, but it wasn't true. I made everybody think that my love for You was something so great, but I know now that it wasn't. I can't be what You want me to be. I'm frail. I'm afraid. I make mistakes. I hurt. I sin. I struggle. There are things inside me that I can't control. Jesus, I'm not the man You and everybody else think I am. I love You, my Lord, but not as deeply as I thought I did.' "

"Peter said all that?" you ask.

"Oh yes," Brokenness answers tenderly. "Peter really got to know me that morning.

"The third time Jesus asked Peter if he loved Him was too much for Peter. I remember him standing in front of Jesus on that beach. When he fell to his knees, I caught him, holding him, supporting him, while he knelt there, a blubbering lump in tears before his Lord. No one spoke for quite some time. I could feel Peter leaning on me more and more as his thoughts screamed at him. *He's asking me again. I can't answer Him. I can't be the mighty man of faith I once thought I was. I'm not perfect. I'm scared. I don't understand.*

"Finally Peter looked up at the Lord and sobbed, 'Lord, You know all things. You know I love You. But I am painfully aware of all the weaknesses that plague me, the sin and failures I struggle with. I'm not sure that I can do what You want me to do.'

"Then Peter turned to me and blurted out, 'Promise me, Brokenness, that you will always stay with me. I have resisted you in the past, and I will probably resist you again in the future, but I know that I need you. Please don't leave me— no matter how much I beg you to go.'

"Jesus said not one word more. He simply took Peter's hand, then mine, and held them in His own.

"Peter and I became good friends that day. For the first time he saw his true self, not who he thought he was or who he wanted others to think he was. He faced his frailty and the weakness that continually assailed him. He confronted his imperfections and his lack of strength. Just as importantly, Peter also discovered that he needed me beside him as his lifelong friend. He asked me to be his constant companion because he knew that he needed Brokenness in his life if he was to have any hope of serving His Lord faithfully.

"You see," Brokenness adds, looking straight into your eyes, "once Peter accepted my friendship and learned to heed my warnings, he discovered that he could obey his Lord despite his struggle to overcome sin and his inability to obey in his own strength. In truth this is the power of Brokenness—the power to repent as often as necessary without shame and without hiding some of the truth. You have nothing to lose, for your Lord knows all about you even before you speak. He is all you need. He is your security; He is your confidence.

"This is what Peter discovered. My continuing friendship radically changed his thoughts, his speech, his actions, and his attitudes. He became a free man.

"Sometimes Peter struggled to maintain his vow to keep me close. In those times I clung to him desperately until he once again embraced me with a genuine thankfulness for my friendship. Soon he began to ask his Lord to change him from the inside. He allowed God to remind him of his failures and his weaknesses."

Brokenness is silent now. Her story is ended. She watches your face to see if you, like Peter, will accept her presence and welcome her influence. She knows that these moments are crucial for you, as significant as those moments on the beach with Jesus were for Peter.

Still you do not speak—perhaps because you are not sure what to say. You know that your heart is softening, but you fear what you might find inside it. In a way, you almost wish that you had never met Brokenness, or at least that you had kept her so far away that she would have no influence over you. Yet you, like Peter, know that you need her.

Silently your eyes give Brokenness permission to stay. Quickly she steps closer until she can enfold you in her arms. As she holds you, Brokenness prays that it will always be so, that you will never have to live without her.

Chapter 6

IN THE ABSENCE OF BROKENNESS

*Only my tears break
the silence of my loneliness.*

T HE COMPANIONSHIP OF BROKENNESS is a bittersweet gift. Though she never purposefully brings you pain, she will not relent when she uncovers a proverbial skeleton as she roots around in the dusty, old corners of the closet in your heart. Faithfully she unveils the ugliness of your rebellion and your insistence on self-determination and draws your attention to the sin that has invaded your humanity. Daily she tries to alert you to compromising situations, point out malignant attitudes, seal your lips from spiteful comments, warn you against possible pitfalls, and unveil some hidden sin in your heart. Always the longing of her heart is to bring healing and restoration.

Her touch is painful at first, and you never grow completely comfortable with her scrutinizing gaze. Still, the more you accept her careful judgment and heed her whispered counsel, the sweeter her presence becomes. You find a wholeness, a sense of fulfillment, and a peace you never dreamed was possible.

Gone are the days of apprehension and withdrawal. You wonder why you once feared her so much. Yes, her searing touch still brings pain and the need for repentance. Yes, her resolute expression when you resist her guidance or when you are slow to respond to her counsel still causes your heart to beat faster. Nevertheless, even then you welcome her presence—perhaps because you have discovered that the companionship of Brokenness brings blessings from your Lord beyond any you have previously received.

It is then, in the midst of this compliant and even complacent friendship, that Brokenness one day whispers a warning. "Beware, lest you ever stop listening to my voice and banish me from your life."

Astonished, you turn to your ever-faithful friend. "Banish you from my life! Haven't I shown you how much I need you? What makes you think that I would choose now to turn away from you? This just doesn't make sense!"

"I have seen it happen many times," Brokenness informs you, with a knowing smile. "Do not be so sure that it cannot happen with you. All I ask is that you be on guard lest you fall into a snare set for you by the evil one."

An absentminded nod is your only response. Brokenness, on the other hand, is not so quick to dismiss the issue.

Urgently she tries to regain your attention. "Do not treat my words so lightly! Surely you have learned how easily impure thoughts, selfish motives, and inconsiderate attitudes can lower your defenses against the invasion of evil."

When you but glance at her quickly before dismissing her pleading words, Brokenness becomes more insistent. "Friend," she entreats you again, "please hear what I am saying! No one is immune to the guiles of the evil one. How stealthily he stalks you! He is always looking for a weakness in your soul that he can prey upon! Listen! Iniquity is a ruthless deceiver. It haunts you, it sticks to you, and ultimately it rules you. Each time you give in to it, you invite the evil one to invade your heart. And where he lives, I cannot. Please be careful. Let nothing come between us!"

"Nothing will separate us," you glibly respond. "I'm sure there is nothing to worry about."

Brokenness is not nearly so convinced of your invincibility as you are. Carefully she increases her vigilance, monitoring your every move. For a time you are quite responsive to her admonitions. Then, as your attentiveness slowly wanes, the day Brokenness warned you about silently arrives.

Oh, how subtly pride slips in unawares! You may not be mindful that you have begun to resist the influence of Brokenness, but she is! At first you are slow to heed her whispered counsel, "Watch out! Be careful!" Then you begin to have less faith in her advice, "Repent! Be careful of this snare the evil one has set for you." Finally you pay little or no attention to her impassioned pleas that fill your soul day and night, trying to bring you to your senses and to warn you of the impending doom that is about to overtake you, "Satan is overwhelming your soul! Turn from this iniquity that has caught you!"

So presumptuous do you become, that you no longer want to even hear what Brokenness has to say. You believe yourself to be beyond her ability to instruct you, to warn you, and to show you the boundaries beyond which many have gone, only to reap the consequences of their prideful attitudes and arrogant self-assurance.

Brokenness observes the ominous signs of her coming exile: the growing suspicion evident in your eyes, the resistance apparent in your posture, and the myriad of expressions that reveal your thoughts and feelings. Soon excuses, words of defense, and even willful accusations begin to pour from your lips.

But Brokenness does not meekly accept your attempts to avoid her. Each time you discount her words, she speaks a little louder, until one day she realizes that she must shout if you are to have any chance of hearing her, so far have you removed yourself from her.

Quickly then she runs to her Lord. "My Lord, my Lord," she calls. "I'm losing influence. My friend no longer heeds my counsel. Please do something quickly. Please bring him to repentance." Even while Brokenness stands before the Lord on your behalf, His voice cracks through the hardness of your heart, calling you to your knees, pleading for you to repent, to open yourself to Brokenness once again. Unfailingly He nudges, prods, and convicts.

Brokenness watches with bated breath as her Lord continues His merciful work, seeking to soften your heart through the words of a trusted friend, the trying circumstances at work, or the insistent voice of a disappointed spouse. Yet she is not content to simply watch. The agony in her heart is far too great for that. Unceasingly she intercedes for you, joining her voice with the groaning of the Holy Spirit, who speaks deep in your heart of this pattern of disobedience that has unfolded in your life. Together they labor for your repentance.

Finally Brokenness notices that you no longer dare to meet her eyes. Disobedience has become such a pattern in your life that she can no longer touch you, even from a distance. Sadly she turns and walks away. You do not even know that she is gone.

Brokenness will not force herself upon you. She would return if she could, but she cannot. Your willful pride and stubborn unrepentance have banished her from your life. With a heavy heart she watches you from afar. Patiently she waits, refusing to beseech her Lord to avert this misery that has come upon you. She has no desire to still His chastening hand.

To the contrary, Brokenness welcomes each trial the Lord sends your way. She recognizes them as His attempts to rescue you, His means of bringing you to repentance, His gifts of love. Though she regrets the pain they bring, she understands that pain is an inevitable part of pride. You cannot live apart from God and avoid pain.

Hopelessness and helplessness overwhelm your heart. Excuses and lies spew from your mouth. One wrong choice after another tightens the knot that makes you a prisoner of the very sin you have so willfully chosen. So great does the weight of this perceived pleasure become that you cannot escape, despite your best efforts to wrestle yourself free.

You are bound, enslaved by your choices to do what you want, when you want, with whom you want, how often you want, in whatever way you want. You have no hope of becoming free—no hope, that is, other than that of the continuing work of God's Spirit deep in your heart. Where there is no repentance, there can be no forgiveness; and where there is no forgiveness, there can be no freedom from sin.

You do not see the hand of your loving Lord in the many crises you face. Instead of turning to Him in repentance, you spend your days blaming others for your misfortunes and rebuking the devil, as though his departure will be the cure-all not only for the sin that has invaded your soul but also for the menacing voice that keeps trying to tell you how guilty you are!

"I rebuke you, satan!" you cry from a heart riddled with pain. "You have no right in my life! I belong to Jesus!"

"Oh, now you belong to Jesus? How convenient!" your enemy replies scornfully, although your ears are too deaf to hear his response to your pitiful prayer.

"Get out of here, you devil!" you shout again. "You have no right on God's property."

"Oh, but I do have a right," the evil one triumphantly replies. "You walked into my camp of your own free will."

"God is my refuge and my strength," you cry belligerently.

"Not here, He isn't," satan denies. "I rule here. If you do not want my counsel, you must leave. Oh, but I forgot, you enjoy the pleasures I offer you. You are not willing to give them up. So I guess you won't be leaving me anytime soon."

Since you are not even aware that he has spoken, your enemy continues in a voice much darker and far more deadly, "You've rejected your God and chosen to stay with me. You are my slave. Get down on your knees and worship me!"

How quickly you would move were your heart open so you could hear the taunts of your enemy. But alas, your heart is not open. You do not—or will not—see that your furious efforts to change the circumstances and avoid the people who appear to be the source of your difficulties are to no avail. Perhaps this is true because you refuse to admit that your attitudes and actions are really sin. Maybe you have no intention of relinquishing the iniquity you hold so dear.

Whatever the cause, day after day you lash out at anyone and everyone who dares to reproach you, including God.

Brokenness grimaces as you attempt to silence the aching call to repentance deep in your heart. She hears your pitiful excuses and your lame attempts at self-justification. "I know exactly what I am doing!" you shout to yourself...to your heart...to whatever is nagging you...perhaps to God. "I know how to run my own life. Why do you keep acting like what I am doing is some big, monstrous sin that is hurting a lot of people? No one is being hurt! I should know!"

Silence follows your tirade, except for the irritating voice inside that relentlessly warns you. *You are so stubborn, you argue back, so sure of yourself and so convinced that I am wrong! Well, I can be just as stubborn. I will not budge!*

Sorrow upon sorrow pierces the heart of Brokenness as she watches you fall more deeply into iniquity. How she yearns for so much as a slight opportunity to rescue you from the brutal hardships that await you; but even now she sees the instruments of bondage and judgment that are ready in the hand of her Lord. Even now she foresees the excruciating pain you will endure as the Lord allows you to experience the slavery you have brought upon yourself.

Bondage is never a place of healing and well-being. God does not intend for it to be. It is a place of captivity, a place where you must bear the inevitable consequences of your stubborn rebellion, your willful disobedience, and your repeated wrong choices. Brokenness cannot help you here;

neither can you warm yourself beneath the approving eyes of your Lord. Desolate and lonely, you must suffer the penalty for your waywardness until repentance springs forth in the desert of your exile.

Chapter 7

THE RETURN OF BROKENNESS

I have found her in my darkness.
She has held me, and I will not let her go.

BONDAGE...JUDGMENT...EXILE...LIFE APART FROM GOD AND THE COMPANIONSHIP OF BROKENNESS. Perhaps you wonder how you came to be here, what path you traveled to warrant such pain. Brokenness asks no such questions. She remembers all too well your descent into iniquity. Every step of your downward spiral is written indelibly on her mind. Yet she has not given up on you. Even now, when you are far beyond her influence, Brokenness still keeps watch over you, waiting for the day when you finally decide that nothing is worth enduring a single moment more of this painful separation.

Daily she beseeches her Lord to do whatever is necessary to break your pride and to bring you to a true understanding of the depth of your sin. Daily she intercedes for you, trusting that the work of the Holy Spirit deep in your heart will move you beyond the ever-present fear that prevents you from facing your weaknesses, the convenient excuses that feed your compulsion to defend your wrong choices, and the mistaken conviction that God neither sees nor cares what you are suffering. Daily she prays that you will soon seek the welcoming embrace of your heavenly Father as you pour out your heart to Him in confession and repentance. Yes, even in the midst of this, your most terrifying pain, Brokenness faithfully looks for some way to touch your heart, to turn you back to your Lord.

As one day passes into another, Brokenness marvels at the severity of discipline with which the Lord woos you. Even your friends draw away from you, sensing that something is amiss. She almost wonders if you have become immune to the work of His Spirit deep in your heart.

Then one day Brokenness notices a slight indication that your calloused conscience is beginning to feel again. Quietly she moves from the shadows and stands where you will see her. The instant you chance to look her way, she holds out her hand to you, inviting you to come to her. Although she would prefer to run to you, taking with her the balm of Gilead, the blessed blood of Jesus, she waits for you to accept her silent invitation.

How surprised you are to see Brokenness standing before you. You have not thought of her for quite some time. Indeed, you are not sure just when she left, but you vaguely remember that you had become tired of her interference. Now here she is confronting you again.

At first you are startled by her stern appearance—it is as though you are meeting her again for the first time. Then you meet her gaze and discover anew the gentle compassion that had once endeared her to you. Confused, you start to look away. Her commanding voice stops you. "Friend, do you remember me?"

"Friend?" you ask weakly. "Did you call me friend?"

"Oh yes," Brokenness responds, taking several steps toward you, "you are my friend. You have never ceased to be my friend. The real question is whether I am your friend."

Do I want her to be my friend? Well, I certainly don't want her around all the time. In fact, I'm not sure I want her around at all.

"Friend," Brokenness persists, "may I tell you a story?"

"Oh no," you respond quickly, "not another story. The last time you told me a story I ended up in your arms! My whole life was changed after that. Nothing was the same. I'm not ready for that again. I think…"

"Friend," Brokenness appeals more softly. "I can help you if you will let me. Don't make your life more difficult than it already is."

"Difficult!" you cry out, with a sound like that of a tormented animal caught in a trap. "What would you know about…?"

You stop and look more closely at Brokenness, scarcely believing what you see. Tears fill her eyes and pain is written on her face.

"What…what is wrong?" you stutter.

"I know what you have suffered," Brokenness reveals, "and I have suffered with you. I can feel the fear that threatens to overwhelm you. You need not face it alone. I can help you. Can you begin by confessing your sin and your hardness of heart? Listen to God's voice and pour out all your fear to Him. He's always ready to listen and forgive."

You are almost willing to throw yourself into the arms of Brokenness, but something holds you back. You are not yet ready to surrender. Perhaps the memories of your first encounters with Brokenness are so frightening that you cannot bear the thought of enduring that torment again. Truly you had vowed that you would never again let her near enough to inflict such pain. Perhaps it is the realization that you do not know how or when your friendship with Brokenness died. Nevertheless, you are unsure whether to surrender or to flee.

Brokenness stands silently beside you, feeling the conflict in your heart. When your silence lengthens and you refuse to meet her eyes, Brokenness quietly asks again, "May I tell you a story about a friend from long ago?"

Again you hesitate. Then you nod almost imperceptibly. Although you long to say no, the nearly suffocating pain in your heart compels you to acquiesce, to give Brokenness a chance to reenter your life.

"Who was this friend?" you ask weakly.

"A shepherd boy who became a king," Brokenness replies, with a look of fond remembrance in her eyes.

"King David?" you mumble, scarcely believing your ears. "Why would you tell me a story about him? He certainly knew nothing of the pain and fear that consume me!"

"Oh, but you are very wrong," Brokenness corrects you gently. "Sometimes David preferred to keep me at a distance, just as you have done. He most certainly was not eager to be my friend when he took his neighbor's wife! Indeed, I had quite a difficult time getting him to admit that he had done anything wrong. Finally, my Lord sent a prophet to show him his sin."

"Yes, I do remember that visit," you respond pensively. "Nathan told David a story. It seems that God is always telling someone a story."

"Yes," Brokenness smiles. "Stories are one of God's favorite ways to teach His children many things. Perhaps it's because stories help us to see ourselves."

"David didn't recognize himself in Nathan's story," you counter.

"No," Brokenness admits. "Nathan had to speak very plainly to David—'You are that man. You have despised the word of the Lord and have done what is evil in His sight'— before he could admit his guilt."

When Brokenness would continue, you stop her, for she need say no more. Your heart, burning with the convicting fire of the Holy Spirit, convinces you that you too have despised the word of the Lord and have done what is evil in His sight. Suddenly you are stunned by what you see in your own heart. You wonder how you came to fall so deeply into sin, to wander so far from obeying God. You recognize the truth of your many weaknesses, struggles, and fears. You see yourself for who you are, who you have become.

Quickly Brokenness steps nearer and pulls you into her arms. With her first touch, the walls you have built around yourself to hide your failures begin to crumble.

"Help me, Brokenness," you sob. "I'm scared by what I see inside myself. I've wandered so far from God that I don't know how I'll ever change. I'm not the person I like to think I am. I'm always struggling with something, and I'm afraid of so much. I struggle to let go of grudges, bad attitudes, and even prejudices. I struggle to trust God. I struggle to obey His voice. I fear the future, wondering what will happen to my job and my family. I fear because there are so many answers that I don't have. How can I go on? How can I even try to go on?"

Brokenness tightens her embrace. "Dear child," she whispers, "I helped David when he faced his struggles and fears. I'll help you too. It's really very simple, you know. Pour out your heart to your Lord. He's yearning to hear your voice again. It's been a long time since you really talked with Him—honestly, that is. I know that the state of your heart shocks you just now, but don't be afraid. God isn't shocked.

He already knows who you are and where you've been. Nothing you tell Him can surprise Him."

"Be gracious to me, O God, according to Your great love and mercy, and forgive my many sins...." Barely do you begin to speak before you sink to the floor, trembling as repentance wells up in your heart. Brokenness kneels beside you, clasping your hand tightly. Though your mind screams for you to pull away from her, you submit to her work. You are so embarrassed, but that is as it should be. Now you see how pride has separated you from the joy of God's presence. Immediately you know that you will do anything to have Him back in your life.

Brokenness pries firmly, yet ever so carefully, at the masks, the coverings, and the facades that became a part of you in the place of your exile. She understands how excruciatingly difficult this is for you. Her finger traces the tears on your face even as your lips confess your sin and admit your need. Her strength supports you as you seek your Lord's mercy and forgiveness. The words flow so freely from your lips. You never believed it would be so easy, so freeing. And when you say to her, "Brokenness, stay with me," a song of joy and thanksgiving wells up in her heart, and worship pure and beautiful pours forth from her lips. Her Lord has used her once again.

Brokenness is again with you, to warn you, to hide you, to remind you of life apart from the power and warmth of God's presence. You lean hard upon her shoulder. Her words of encouragement fill your ears. Long after you forget the details of this day, you will remember the gentle assurance that urges you to take the road of Brokenness. It is a road of confession and quiet humility, a road from which flow the mighty rivers of God's love to your family, your community, and the nations. Feebly at first, then with more confidence, you step out to walk this road again.

Brokenness rejoices before her Lord. Although she knows that there will be days ahead when you will not be so willing to have her near you—you may even choose to banish her again—it is enough that she is here with you now. Her silent vigil, her time of exile, has ended. Now she must begin to renew her friendship with you, a friendship built upon repentance and surrender.

Chapter 8

LIVING WITH BROKENNESS

*I am embarrassed to remember life without
her wisdom. I have hidden myself in her.*

DAYS HAVE PASSED. YOU LIE IN THE ARMS OF BROKEN-
NESS, spent by your weeping and the pain you
have suffered.

"Do you understand what happened to bring you to
these terrible days?" Brokenness questions you quietly.

"I disobeyed God," you respond weakly but quickly, a
sure sign that Brokenness is truly being planted in your
heart. You are not surprised that Brokenness should ask
such a question. In truth, you are beginning to understand
that these questions serve to check your spirit and to confirm your willingness to be honest when they expose something in you that you may have ignored.

"Yes, you disobeyed God," Brokenness affirms, "but
you have disobeyed God in the past without coming to

this crossroads. Do you understand what was different about this experience?"

You look intently into the eyes of Brokenness, trying to understand what she is asking. You have no doubt that you have sinned greatly, but Brokenness seems to be looking for something far more basic than the details of your sin.

Brokenness leans closer. "Do you remember the days when we were good friends?" You nod, although the memory of that long-ago time is dim and unclear. "Sometimes we talked for hours," Brokenness reminds you, "and you were so quick to respond to my counsel. Even when we didn't have much time to talk, I had only to look at you, or to touch you lightly on the shoulder, and you quickly acknowledged my presence and turned to embrace me. Your heart was soft and pliable. You had no greater pleasure than hearing and obeying the voice of your Lord. Time and time again you were free to confess your sin, to acknowledge your humanity, and to desperately embrace your Lord, who is always ready to forgive, empower, and guide.

"Then came the day when you stopped fighting. You allowed the invader of your humanity, that old devil, to reestablish his control in your life. For a time you tried to live under his authority and the authority of the Lord Jesus—acting one way at church and another way at home, one way in private and another way in public. You tried to put on the nature of Christ when it suited you and to hide it whenever you preferred to act on your own authority, or that of your enemy.

"I tried so hard to show you the change in your heart, but you were not willing to hear me. You would not believe that you were changing your lifestyle, setting aside your Lord's choice to follow your own. You would not admit, or even see, that you were again trying to rule your life. Nevertheless, that is what happened.

"In the beginning, when your inclination to choose your own way began to increase, I tried to remind you that you had made Jesus the Lord of your life. Each time you started to take control, I whispered, 'You have nothing to hold on to. You've given everything to Jesus. Just do whatever He asks. Be careful to listen for His voice.' Before long I had to shout so that you could hear me."

You look at Brokenness with amazement. You don't remember any of this. *Could I have been so callous?* you wonder. *Why was I so unready to believe my friend?*

"Do you know why I changed?" you ask Brokenness.

"Yes, I can tell you what went wrong. Better yet, I can show you exactly when you made the choice to…"

"I chose to change?" you interrupt, not sure for the first time if you believe her.

"Oh yes," Brokenness affirms. "I clearly remember the day you chose to follow your own will instead of obeying God."

You sit in silent disbelief as Brokenness unfolds a tale of repeated disobedience and rebellion that began with a single choice to willfully do what you knew to be sin. You remember the day and the choice as soon as she mentions them.

Your heart had indeed condemned you that day—and even more so in the days that followed as you tried to excuse your behavior. You even recall the disapproving look Brokenness gave you before you turned your back on her, dismissing her words as so much nonsense.

Now you realize how right Brokenness was. Her words that day, "Are you forgetting that Jesus Christ is your Lord?" flood your mind and pierce your very soul as you admit that this is precisely what you did. Because you were not willing to set aside your plans to do what your Lord wanted, you opened the door for the great deceiver to enter your heart and start you on a journey of pain and misery.

"Not only your one deliberate act of disobedience but also your persistent stubbornness that would not permit you to admit your wrong brought you to this painful time," Brokenness continues. "You allowed yourself to drift into the deadly pattern of choosing when Jesus would be your Lord and when you would claim that right for yourself.

"The more frequently you chose to make yourself king over your life, the farther away you pushed me. When you no longer even tried to put God's will over your own, you sent me into exile and our relationship was severed. For a time, I could not even talk to you or approach you because you had so given yourself over to doing exactly what you wanted, when you wanted, and how you wanted."

Brokenness tightens her grip on your hand. You lift your head to glance at her face. You are surprised to see tears pouring down her cheeks. In that moment, you see that Brokenness has suffered every bit as much as you have.

"I'm sorry," you whisper as tears fill your eyes. "I had no idea."

Brokenness smiles at you through her tears. Memories of days gone by filter through your mind. You remember the years when you had given yourself to Jesus, allowing His anointing to flow through you. How easy it was early in your life with the Lord when His love bubbled freely from your heart, effortlessly filling all your days. You wonder why this effervescence of His presence and power did not continue.

"God wants His love to bubble freely again in your life," Brokenness continues. "He longs for you to bask in the warmth of His love as you did when you first came to Him. It is a lie that the effect of His love lessens with age or familiarity. The more familiar you become with Him, the more His love should affect you. As time passes, your love and exuberance for His presence should grow, not diminish."

Now your grip tightens on the hand of Brokenness. You wonder if you can face what lies ahead. Brokenness feels your uncertainty. "Don't be afraid," she consoles you. "The way before you may be difficult, but I will walk every step with you. Lean on my strength. Keep your ears attuned to my voice. Trust the heart of your Lord. Be quick to confess your sin.

"You cannot have the benefits of God's power while sin still rules your heart. Sharing His blessings demands that you surrender completely to His Lordship. You must allow me to touch the hardness of your heart before you can experience God's power flowing through you freely and unrestricted."

"I have to give up my lordship to Christ's Lordship." You speak softly, as though you are settling in your mind what you know in your heart to be true. "I have to resist the invasion of sin in me each and every day. I have to give up my personal rights if I want to follow my Lord."

Suddenly your rights do not seem so important. Indeed, looking into the heart of Brokenness, your rights appear so naive, so immature. It's almost embarrassing. God's plan is so far above your puny attempts to maintain control of your life. "I am ready, Lord," you pray. "Free me from this sin."

Brokenness nods in agreement when you turn to her with a trembling smile. "Are you ready to go on?" she asks, her soft voice filled with gentle compassion.

When you talk to Brokenness of your prayer, she assures you that others have learned the lesson that awaits you. "You are not the first person to face this difficult decision. I have taught many others how to yield to God's will instead of insisting on their own way."

Now you see what happens when you choose your own way. You know that you have no other place to turn. One day, if you cling to her, Brokenness will bring you to the point where you are willing to do anything to do the will of God. Nothing will be too difficult or too unusual. No command will be impossible. Until then you set your face to walk with Brokenness, learning the pain and joy of her companionship and allowing yourself to discover her spirit.

Chapter 9

THE SPIRIT OF BROKENNESS

She sees in me things that I cannot see—
faithful things, wonderful things, loving things.

BROKENNESS smiles as you join her early one morning. She seems to enjoy these opportunities to share her life with you and to lead you closer to the Father's heart. This morning she walks in silence, perhaps because she knows that you still need time to adjust to your new way of living.

Over the past days since Brokenness reentered your life, she has shown you a clearer picture of yourself than you have seen for quite some time. Reluctantly at first, then with more openness, you have allowed her to unveil the many relationships and situations in your life that reveal the magnitude of sin's invasion in your heart. Many times you have found yourself on your knees in repentance, sometimes several times a day. Confession has poured from your lips and tears of repentance have given you such a wonderful relief as the blood of Jesus has washed away bitterness, anger, jealousy, and a host of other invaders.

Through all this Brokenness has held you close. The memory of the gentleness in her fingers as they wiped away your tears comforts you. You can almost feel her hand upon you, as if in benediction. You glance at her, wondering where she might lead you today. You find her kind eyes upon you, almost as if she is waiting for you to speak.

"My friend," Brokenness says, drawing closer to you, "the days since we again began walking together have been extremely difficult for you. I know you have struggled to accept all that I have shown you. The days ahead need not be so distressing. How much you suffer depends on the spirit with which you walk with me. Yes, there are still willful strongholds in your heart that you must surrender to your Lord, but be careful that you do not try to change these by yourself. God intends for you to work with Him, not for Him. He'll bring new life to your heart if you'll just choose to surrender to His will. Surrendering your will to God's will is very similar to a seed's surrendering its life for a greater purpose."

Pausing, Brokenness leads you to the shade of a large tree and invites you to sit with her. Picking up a seed of the great oak tree, she begins to teach you about an eternal paradox. "Death is the prerequisite for life. It is the process through which life arises. This seed must give itself completely to the ground before a new tree can sprout and grow. Only in its death can it be reborn to a more splendid life. If the seed does not die, a new tree is impossible. Without surrender, the magnificence of the tree and all the fruit it will bear in its lifetime are lost.

"The same principle can be applied to your life. If you see death to self as defeat, you will not die to yourself; but if you see death as the gateway to new life, you will fervently, though at times painfully, embrace its pathway. Likewise, if you walk with me in a spirit of openness, you will find great joy and victory in the journey. One day, after you have learned to set your focus on your Lord and the joy of pleasing Him, you will find that dying to yourself even becomes sweet."

"How long will we walk together like this?" you ask, searching the face of Brokenness as you await her answer.

"The rest of your life...or until you banish me again," she replies.

"Until I banish you again?" you repeat in a voice filled with the anguish that suddenly pierces your heart. "I never want to banish you again!"

"I am glad to hear this, my friend," Brokenness whispers softly. "I know that you are very aware of the sin that has caused you so much pain, but be careful lest you believe that nothing else in your life is so bad that God must put you through trying times again. You see yourself from the outside, but God sees your heart.

"He sees the pride that keeps you from admitting your weaknesses and your need to depend on Him. Yet, in His mercy, He will not show you the true state of your heart all at once. He knows that you would become too discouraged to go on. All God asks is that you let me be your lifelong companion so He can show you who you are and who you were made to be.

"The longer you walk with me, the more you will discover who God created you to be. That's as it should be," Brokenness continues. "His anointing is not available to the highest bidder. His power is revealed only in those who choose to empty themselves so that He can fill them. Each time you choose to relinquish whatever stands in the way of your obeying Him, a little more of His power oozes through the cracks in your self-sufficiency and your self-will. As you continue to yield your will to your Lord's will, sin is driven more fully from a place of influence and infection in your life.

"God covers those who repent and exposes those who cover their sin," Brokenness adds. "This is another eternal paradox. When you admit your sin, your failures, your shortcomings, your wrong attitudes, your spiteful thoughts, and your inappropriate responses—anything that shows you are putting your ego above God's will—the blood of Jesus covers your sin until it can cleanse you. Therefore the world sees only Jesus.

"On the other hand, whenever you hide your sin, God must first bring you to repentance before He can cover you. Sometimes He uncovers your sin before the world, using the shame of exposure as part of His work in your heart. He would prefer to teach and chasten you privately, but He will do so publicly if you do not respond to the gentle conviction of His Holy Spirit. To your Lord, your relationship with Him is infinitely more important—and definitely more eternal in consequence—than your reputation or any discomfort you may feel.

"The measures God uses to show you your sin are directly related to how teachable you are. You can learn to be sensitive to the direction and discipline of the Lord, heeding His commandments and obeying His voice as soon as you hear it."

"What if I'm not ready to respond to your voice or the gentle nudge of the Holy Spirit? What happens then?" you ask.

"There certainly are times when God wants to say something to you that you don't want to hear," Brokenness agrees. "If our friendship is warm and open, you will find that I quiet your heart and give you the grace to hear and obey.

"You must remember," Brokenness continues, "that God is the great I AM. He uses the now to prepare you for tomorrow. Now is all He has to mold you for whatever your future holds. The more you resist Him now, the longer the preparation will take.

"So when you hear the voice of your Lord, be careful not to harden your heart. He is committed to dealing with you today. Whenever His hand of discipline touches your life, He is always trying either to correct some sin that has crept into your heart or to lead you in a new direction.

"This is the spirit of Brokenness. Your hunger to hear and obey God's word to you outweighs the momentary pleasure of insisting on your own way. You intentionally choose death to your selfish choices so that the life of Christ can arise within your heart. As you surrender yourself to your Lord day after day, you learn how to give yourself over to God's dream for you. Sometimes this cooperation with God is difficult. Nevertheless, if you trust Him, you will eventually find that you can wait for Him or move with Him, whichever is required. Brokenness leads you to surrender your will to God's will so you can be a part of His master plan for the planet."

Chapter 10

BROKENNESS WAITS FOR GOD

"Patience, my noble one," I hear her whisper to me.
"The night is very dark. So do not run ahead of your light."

BROKENNESS waits for you in the secluded cove that has become your special meeting place. You have come to look forward to these trysts when you review the past few days and seek her counsel on what you will face during the day that is just beginning to dawn. Responding to her gentle touch has become easier since you set aside this time to talk before you rush into the day.

Today your feet drag as you walk to your special place. You are discouraged, worn down by the unending monotony of the same routines, the same people, and the same responsibilities. It's not that your life is so terribly bad. It merely seems to have no purpose, as though God has abandoned His dream for you.

Brokenness looks up at the sound of your footsteps. She greets you warmly, then steps closer to examine your face. "What's wrong, my friend?" she asks quietly. "You don't look very happy this morning."

You turn your head to meet her eyes, welcoming her genuine concern. "I don't really know."

"Has something happened to upset you?" she inquires.

"No, not really."

"Well, how long have you felt this way?"

"I haven't been content for quite a while. It seems that my life isn't going anywhere."

"You remind me of a young man I once befriended. He too struggled with disillusionment and a sense that God had somehow forgotten him. As a boy he had received two remarkable visions from the Lord, but once he became a young man nothing seemed to come of them. I can still hear Joseph complain, 'When is God going to get around to doing what He showed me?' "

You look at Brokenness with little interest. You already know this story, but you know better than to protest. You seldom win against Brokenness, since she is one persistent female and is always right. So you sit in the soft grass of this tiny cove and lean against a tree, nodding courteously for her to go on.

"I followed Joseph from the days of his boyhood, talking to him and encouraging him to wait on the Lord. I remember well that first night after Joseph had been thrown into

Pharaoh's prison. I found him crying himself to sleep in a far corner of that dark and lonely cell. When I touched his arm, he pulled away from me, mumbling in a bewildered, but quite angry voice. 'What are *you* doing here? You sure had me fooled. How stupid I was to believe you! "Cling to me!" you said. "Trust the Lord!" you said. "God will vindicate you!" you said. This doesn't look like vindication or God's guidance to me. Is this the high tower you always talk about? Is this the green pasture God promised me?'

"Joseph buried his face in his hands, engulfed in his sorrow. The next few weeks were the most difficult times we suffered through in our many years of friendship. One moment Joseph thought that God had forsaken him, and the next he complained that God must be angry with him.

" 'Why doesn't God rescue me?' he whined to me. 'He's forgotten me, that's why. He doesn't even remember that I'm alive.'

" 'You know that's not true,' I admonished him. 'You have to accept that God sees from a perspective you don't see—at least not yet. You have to be patient. At the right time, He will vindicate you. Please don't rush ahead of Him. It never works to try to out-maneuver your Lord.'

" 'Patient?' Joseph exclaimed. 'Day after day I do whatever the jailer asks me to do, hoping that good behavior will get me out of here, but I'm still here.'

" 'Perhaps God is trying to teach you something,' I suggested. 'You must admit that your attitude has been pretty dismal lately. If you would change your attitude, you would find that your time here is more tolerable. Only you can choose to make the best of this situation and to trust that God will work things out when He is ready. The only other way is to allow your anger and frustration to derail you from God's dream for your life.'

" 'Remember, Joseph, no person or circumstance can thwart God's plans. When He's ready to move, things will change. Until then, no amount of conniving can help you. Oh, you may find a way to change your situation, but if you're not careful, you'll find that you get to your goal before God does, which is quite the same as not arriving at your goal at all.'

" 'That's impossible! I can't get to my destiny before God does because I don't have a destiny. God's completely forgotten the dreams He gave me.'

" 'Don't be too sure of that, young man,' I warned Joseph sternly. 'Why don't you just work at doing a good job where you are and let God sort out when it's time for a promotion. He'll be faithful to you, you can be sure of that. The real question is, will He find you being faithful to Him when He comes to deliver you?'

"Joseph turned and walked away. I had no doubt that he wanted to be alone. Maybe he was tired of me chastising him all the time, but I couldn't let him stop trusting God. Too much was at stake.

"The time alone must have changed something in Joseph's heart. The next morning he greeted me with a smile. Then he apologized: 'I'm sorry I've been so grouchy lately. I'm afraid I forgot how to look beyond my circumstances to what God is doing. Sometimes it seems like the whole world is passing by and here I am, stuck in an obscure prison with no future. I can't do anything I want to do, and nobody knows I am here. Worst of all, I doubt if even one person cares what is happening to me. Nonetheless, I really do know better. I know that I must wait for my Lord! I want His will for my life, even if I gripe about it too much.'

" 'It's easy to look only at the difficult things that surround you,' I conceded, 'but remember, the process of getting to your goal is just as important as the goal itself. If you hurry the process or avoid it altogether, you won't be ready when you do finally reach your destination. The ultimate success of fulfilling your destiny is intricately tied to your submission to the process and the timetable.'

"That wasn't the last time Joseph was tempted to give up on the dreams God had given him or to hurry the process of reaching his destiny," Brokenness continues, shifting her position on the ground, "but it was definitely a turning point in his life. After that, whenever he became caught up in remembering the injustices he had suffered or the long spans when he seemed to have been forgotten, I had only to call his attention to his attitude before he quickly repented and trusted God again."

"How sad it would have been had Joseph forfeited his destiny," you add. "The course of history would have been changed."

"Yes," Brokenness concurs, "but think of the tragedy if he had reached his destiny before he had learned the lessons

God planned for him. His positions as the manager of Potiphar's household and the supervisor in the prison were important training grounds for the skills he would need as Pharaoh's right-hand man."

"So maybe I'm in training right now for something God has planned for me," you suggest.

"That's entirely possible," Brokenness agrees. "So you'd better be careful to learn what you're supposed to learn now so that you are prepared when that time comes. Set your eyes on Him alone, and you'll find that life regains a new purpose and interest for you.

"God's always working for your good. Nothing He sends your way is random or haphazard. Beneath the minor irritants—the difficult people, complicated situations, and discouraging circumstances you face every day—He has set in motion a plan to bring you into the fullness of all He created you to be. Depend on Him to show you each step of the plan when He is ready."

Brokenness pauses and looks intently into your eyes before she continues. "He will not leave you behind. He sees your talents, your gifts, and your heart to serve. So be content where He has you, even if He has put you in hiding, where no one sees you, no one recognizes your gifts, and no one seems to care. God sees, especially when He is silent. I know. I am sure He sees you. Again and again I have seen Him unfold His plans. Trust Him to work for you too. Trust Him moment by moment, being careful not to promote yourself no matter how tempting that possibility might become.

"Oh yes, in the meantime, when it seems that nothing is happening and you are stuck in the same old place, check your attitude and adjust it where necessary. Then do with all your heart everything you are given to do. It doesn't matter how simple or how demeaning these tasks might seem to be; do them and do them well. Only your pride will be challenged by their smallness, and we both know what has to happen to that."

For many minutes you say nothing. Your heart has been strangely stirred by these words from Brokenness. Perhaps her story has caught your heart because you now realize that there are people in your life whom you resent too. Soon you begin praying for those you have secretly condemned. Now you know that you are in competition with no one. Should God choose to move someone ahead of you, or to give another the recognition or promotion you think you deserve, you can truly rejoice with him, knowing that God has not forgotten you. Your times are in His hands, and He does not forget or arrive too late. Your destiny cannot be lost by the advancement of another.

Repentance fills your heart as you confess the wrong attitudes that have kept you from loving these people. You are free to encourage them toward their destiny without being threatened by their advancement. You are also free to wait for God's recognition and God's timing. Gradually your heart is warmed.

Yes, obscurity is good, even excellent, when it is the place of God's choosing. It is a safe place—a place of learning, a place to gain new strength. So you relax, letting God open or close the doors in your life. You are certain that there is no reason to fret. Today is the Lord's, as is tomorrow. Whatever He sends your way will be precisely what you need. Yes, for the first time in your life, you can truly trust God with your future, your career, your destiny—indeed your entire life.

Chapter 11

BROKENNESS MOVES WITH GOD

It is not the hearing that impedes
my going, it is the fear of doing.

B ROKENNESS has now been your companion for a very long time. As the years slip by, you wonder how you ever lived without her. Yes, there are still times when you find her nearness exasperating and even troubling, but you have come to value her counsel and the clarity with which she shows you the sinful attitudes that prevent you from obeying God completely, willingly, immediately.

You are truly at peace with your faithful companion—now that you are learning to repent more quickly—and also at peace with yourself. The excuses, masks, and self-justification that were once regular patterns in your life are gone. Oh, you most definitely have not arrived—of that you are painfully aware. Almost daily Brokenness uncovers some hidden pocket of resistance that prevents you from maturing as rapidly as you would prefer. Still, life with Brokenness has become much more tolerable. You find it easier to respond to her gentle touch. No longer are you surprised or terrified by what she might find. So you respond warmly when Brokenness greets you early one morning.

"What's on your mind this morning?" you ask, sitting down beside her.

"How different this is from the early days when we were just beginning to get acquainted," Brokenness says. "You always suspected then that I was trying to make trouble for you."

"Yes," you agree with a smile, "I was never quite sure what you were going to do next and what it was going to cost me. We've come a long way together. I still don't like some of the things you tell me, but at least I'm not afraid that you are trying to destroy me. I think I have you figured out. You're just an old softy under all your calculated coldness."

"Oh, do you think so?" Brokenness scoffs. "We'll see if you still feel that way after I'm done with you today!"

Quickly you glance into the eyes of Brokenness. How relieved you are to see laughter there. "You had me scared for a minute," you confess. "I was afraid that I had spoken too soon."

"I have another story to tell you," Brokenness says.

You smile to yourself. You are quite used to her stories by now. Today you are curious, even eager, to hear what Brokenness has to say.

"As a young man, Moses had an inkling that he was supposed to be a deliverer. The only problem was that no one but Moses, and God of course, had the slightest idea of this calling. The Hebrews didn't know, and Pharaoh certainly didn't recognize it, so nobody expected that Moses would one day suddenly decide to act like a deliverer when he saw an Egyptian beating a Hebrew slave.

"When his efforts didn't have the intended effect, Moses became frightened and ran to the wilderness. There he spent 40 years tending sheep, 40 years of apparent failure, far from his destiny. Moses didn't know it when he ran to the wilderness, but that was exactly where God wanted him to be, and I was there waiting for him.

"Some of those years were very difficult for Moses as I brought him face-to-face with himself. Many times he would have been quite content to send me to another part of the country. Nevertheless, we became friends.

"One day, 40 years after Moses had enjoyed the splendor and glory of being raised in the Pharaoh's house, the mighty deliverer of Israel, wearing sheep skins instead of the finest linen, was warming himself beside a fire of sheep clods. The wealth of Egypt was no longer at his disposal. Instead he shared the relative poverty of the family into which he had married. To this Moses, God was about to speak through a smoking clump of brush on an obscure Midianite hillside.

" 'Moses!'

" 'Yes?' Moses gulped, looking at me quickly to see if I had also heard the voice.

" 'I need you to go on an errand for Me. I'm sending you to Pharaoh to free My people from the tyranny of Egypt. I want you to deliver them.'

" 'An errand?' Moses turned to me, a bit confused. 'You want me to...to go on an errand for You?' he stammered. 'You must be kidding! How can I go to Egypt and be a deliverer?'

" 'You are the one I am sending,' God replied, 'and I'll go with you.'

"Moses was so stunned that he dropped his staff. I had to steady him then or he would have fallen.

" 'But I don't even know who You are,' Moses protested again, gesturing wildly for me to intervene.

" 'I'll give you miraculous signs, Moses, so that you will know that I really am with you. After you've freed My people, you'll come back here to this mountain to worship Me.'

" 'But who are You...what's Your name?' Moses asked frantically. 'What shall I tell the people when they ask who sent me?'

" 'Tell them I AM WHO I AM sent you.'

" 'But what if they don't believe me?' Moses objected yet again. 'What if they won't listen to what I say?' I rolled my eyes and poked Moses in the ribs with my elbow when I heard this excuse falling from his lips. He was so intent on avoiding God's orders that he acted like I wasn't even there.

" 'Stop making excuses and trying to get out of what I'm requiring you to do,' God demanded, making it apparent that He was not going to let Moses escape from obeying His word. 'I'll tell you what to say and I'll help you to say it.'

"Finally Moses, seeing how quickly his objections had been overruled, blurted out, 'Please, God, I can't do this. Just send someone else.'

"I couldn't believe my ears," Brokenness admits. "I just glared at Moses. After all the years of our friendship, there he was telling his Creator God that he wouldn't accept the assignment!

" 'Okay, Moses. I'll send your brother Aaron with you. He's a good speaker, but you must tell him what to say. I will speak to you, and you will give him My words. Now stop whining and go! And here, don't forget your staff!' "

When Brokenness finishes her story, you wait for her to speak again. You don't understand why she has related this experience from Moses' life, so you are caught off guard when she asks you, "Do you recognize yourself in this story?"

"Well...I don't understand what you mean."

"How many times have you refused to do what God wanted you to do because you didn't believe that you could do it?" Brokenness persists.

"A few," you reply.

"A few? Think again! God has so much that He wants to do through you, but you are just like Moses. You are reluctant to trust Him."

"I don't hear God asking me to do anything great and mighty like He asked Moses to do," you protest. "In fact, I'm not aware of anything He's asked me to do that I haven't done."

"I guess I have more work ahead of me than I realized," Brokenness comments, more to herself than to you. "Let's go back a few steps."

You tap your fingers against your leg as you fight the sinking feeling that you have missed something major. Although you do not understand what Brokenness means, the tone of her voice makes you nervous.

"Do you remember when I first convinced you that God has a dream for your life?" Brokenness asks, scanning your face to be sure that you understand her question.

"Of course," you reply.

"Well, that dream is never going to come true unless you come into alignment with what He has already purposed in His heart for your destiny. God did not just determine your destiny, He prepared a pathway to see its fulfillment. In fact, this pathway is the only way you will fulfill His dreams for you. You may not understand the whole plan He has laid out for your life, but surely you are aware of some doors He has already opened."

Slowly you nod in agreement. *Yes, that's true*, you think to yourself. *I have caught tiny glimpses of where God might take me someday.*

"Now you must obediently walk through every door He opens for you," Brokenness advises you. "The issue is never God's unwillingness to direct you. It is always your unwillingness to walk through the doors He opens, to accept whatever assignment He gives you, and to take every opportunity He sends your way to prepare you for the future. If you don't see His moving in your life, it's probably because He's already asked you to do something that you have not yet done, and He's waiting for you to obey."

"What if I'm not sure that the dreams in my heart are God's dreams?" you ask.

"Start acting on them and you'll soon find out," Brokenness replies. "If they are truly God's dreams, you'll discover that your horizons expand as you obey Him. It doesn't matter how ridiculous, how difficult, or how threatening His propositions appear to be, you must obey His voice if you want Him to lead you into the next step."

Still trying to avoid the issue, you continue to whine, "What if I'm not comfortable with what I feel God is asking me to do?"

"This sounds familiar, doesn't it? It's precisely the problem Moses had."

"I guess it is," you admit slowly, realizing for the first time how much like Moses you really are.

"Your excuses are no more acceptable than his were. Neither should you expect to tell God how to do the job He's giving you to do. If you try to tell God what to do, you will find that He is no more agreeable to your suggestions than Jesus was to the tempter's suggestions in the wilderness.

"God doesn't need you to tell Him how to order your life," Brokenness admonishes you. "In fact, He doesn't even require that you tell Him what you need. Your assessment may be completely wrong. What God does need is your willingness to do whatever He asks, to go wherever He sends you, and to try anything He gives you a heart to do, even if you think you cannot do it. He needs you to pray daily, 'God, I'm here. Do what You want with me. I'm open to Your touch. Help me to hear Your voice and to see what You are doing. I'm willing to serve You, Lord. I'm ready to go. Where I am not willing, please change my heart.' "

You look at Brokenness with increasing understanding. "That's what you do, isn't it?" you exclaim.

"Yes," Brokenness agrees. "Nothing gives me greater pleasure than hearing the voice of my Lord and doing whatever He asks as soon as He requires it."

"I don't think I've learned this eager obedience yet."

"No, but you will learn it if you stick with me. I'll open your ears to the voice of God and I'll help you to take some risks."

"Risks?"

"Yes, risks. What God wants you to do may not always fit with the assumptions and expectations of others. There is no guarantee that they will accept what you do.

"Even then your primary concern must be to obey your Lord. Do what He asks. You are His bond slave. It is Him you must please. In truth, you have nothing to lose and much to gain by your obedience.

"You see, the risk of disobeying God is much greater than the consequence of not obeying Him for fear that you may offend someone. God is always faithful to those who obey Him. He will accomplish His purposes for your life despite the opinions and judgments of those who scorn your obedience.

"Fearing God more than man is the key to your destiny. Then when God is ready to move, you will be ready to move, and an environment of possibilities is created. You're free to cooperate with whatever God is doing without shutting Him up in a box formed by your preconceived ideas. He can send you on an assignment much more incredible than you would ever dare to imagine, simply because you are ready to move or wait as He directs. Your choice to obey Him no matter how preposterous His plan may seem to be is what enables you to experience the exhilarating freedom and power of aligning yourself with God."

Chapter 12

THE SCHOOL OF BROKENNESS

I have embraced her way of life: to treasure
what others disdain, to love what others scorn.

L IFE WITH BROKENNESS grows even sweeter as the
years pass. You have learned so many things. You
know that your heart is changing. In a way, it's strange.
Things that used to be so difficult are becoming easier. Even
your thoughts are changing. Where before your favorite pas-
time was to review how certain people were responsible for
many of the problems you have had to face, now you find
yourself praying for the very people you have criticized. You
are consumed much less frequently by bitterness and the
pleasures of fantasizing about your alleged enemies and their
soon-coming fall from grace. A divorce, a business failure,
the sudden loss of a job—how you loved to meditate on your
perceived enemy's possible demise. It didn't really matter

what the circumstance, as long as the demise was devastating and most definitely hurt…really hurt.

Now Brokenness has changed all that. Leaning strongly on her has allowed you to see yourself, including the errors and impatience that wrought most of your more serious dilemmas. Repentance flows from your lips as you recognize the friendships you have lost and the vast amounts of time you have wasted blaming others for what was most certainly your fault. Bitterness that has ruled your heart for years begins to fall away like so many leaves falling from an oak tree on a brisk autumn afternoon.

Often you walk in silent companionship with Brokenness. There is no need to converse. When your heart is soft, as it is many days now, your communication is heart to heart. You feel your need, and you know her response. Your repentance opens the door of God's grace and gives you the power to go on.

One day, you come upon a person lying in the dust by the side of the road. His face is streaked by the tears that mingle with the dust on his face, and his chest heaves from the effort of his travail. You recognize immediately that this could be you were Brokenness not your companion.

"Poor fellow," Brokenness murmurs as she stoops to help the stricken man. When the man arouses from his misery long enough to pull away from her, Brokenness whispers to you, "How I wish he would let me help him. Not long ago he was strutting along with great pride. I warned him that he would soon fall, but he would not heed my cry. In fact, he has been so sure of himself that he has repeatedly snubbed me.

"In many ways he reminds me of another traveler I met one day. He too was very proud and very sure of himself. We later became good friends, but it sure took a while."

"Who was this person?" you ask curiously.

Brokenness chuckles. "Some of my first conversations with him were closer to arguments," Brokenness confesses rather sheepishly, knowing that she is not supposed to argue with anyone, "but we really did become longtime friends. He was Saul, Saul of Tarsus."

"Do you mean the apostle Paul?"

"Yes, that's the man, although I first knew him as Saul of Tarsus. He led me on quite a chase before I finally caught up with him."

"What do you mean?" you exclaim, still unable to believe that you are talking about the same person. "Paul was always so obedient to God. Nothing was too much to suffer for his Lord. Boat crashes, beatings, imprisonments, money troubles, rejection. He suffered much because of his faithfulness to the Lord. Many times he went without food, and lots of times he couldn't find a place to sleep and he didn't have decent clothes to wear. More than that, he spent most of his life on the brink of assassination because he obeyed his Lord."

"Yes, I know what you have believed about the apostle Paul, but Saul certainly wasn't that kind of man all those early years I trailed him, trying to get his attention. It was only after he became like this unfortunate man lying by the side of the road…"

"What?" you interrupt. "Are you saying that you had something to do with his conversion, with the fall from his horse?"

Brokenness nods as she remembers that morning.

"Oh my!" you reply, more than a little surprised. "You really do go where no man has gone before!"

"You have no idea…but that's not the important thing here," Brokenness answers, working to get the conversation back on track. "The important thing is that Saul was just like this man."

"Paul was like this man? This man won't make it through the day. Paul never had a day like this poor guy is having, and he certainly was never in this state."

"That's what you think! Were Saul here now he would tell you about the day his world turned upside down. If ever a man was confused and discouraged, it was Saul the day he met Jesus."

"But Paul was so confident and so powerful," you argue. "He always seemed to have the right answer and to be exactly where God wanted him to be." You pause, shaking your head. "You know, I find all this very hard to believe."

"There was no doubt of Saul's condition that day long ago on the Damascus Road. I stood nearby, watching as everything he had believed and lived for crumbled before his eyes. He was terribly frightened."

When you would interrupt her yet again, Brokenness lifts her hand to silence your words. "I know you have difficulty believing this, but your picture of Paul is influenced by many, many opinions of generation after generation of Church scholars and theologians. These are not even close to accurately describing the man I caught up with on the road to Damascus.

"Yes, there were times when Paul was a man of great strength and power who risked a lot and suffered a lot to obey God; but that wasn't always true. In fact, in the beginning of my acquaintance with Saul, he was too full of himself to hear God, let alone obey Him. But by the end of his life, Saul believed that he needed more of God's grace and mercy than absolutely anyone else in history.

"I was Saul's adversary that fateful day on the road to Damascus. There he was, lying on the road, angry and confused. Yet his pride was too great to let anyone come to his aid. I can still see him struggling to his feet, angrily shaking off the hands that tried to help him stand.

"The next morning I watched Saul as he lay sleeping on the floor. The stain of tears still streaked his face. His clothes and hair were rumpled, giving him an unkempt appearance that was quite foreign to him. He scarcely looked like the man I'd pursued for so many months.

"When he began to stir, I watched him intently, eager to see how he would respond once he woke up. At first he simply lay there, his hands limp at his sides, as though he was trying to wake up enough to know where he was. Suddenly the stillness was rent by a frenzied cry of incredible pain and disbelief.

" 'My God,' Saul cried, the torment in his soul showing clearly in the tone of his voice. 'I am still blind. It was not a dream. It really happened. Is anybody here? Does anybody even care that I cannot see? Where are my friends? What happened to the guards?'

"Wearily Saul stood and groped around until he found a chair. His expression matched the mood of his grumbling. I took a deep breath and prepared to greet him. When we first arrived in Damascus, I did not tell Saul that I was there with him. I knew that he was not ready to appreciate my nearness.

" 'Hello, Saul,' I greeted him quietly.

" 'You!' he exclaimed, standing up so quickly that he overturned the chair on which he had been sitting. 'What are you doing here? I suppose you have come to gloat over my misery. I thought I told you to stop pestering me.'

" 'Yes, that is true,' I agreed calmly. 'That is why you were met on the road by my Lord, Jesus.'

" 'What do you mean?' Saul exclaimed, turning toward the sound of my voice. 'What has Jesus to do with you?'

" 'He is my Lord,' I answered humbly. 'I have been following you and approaching you at His request. When you would not let me get near you, I ran for His help. He confronted you on the road because you would not respond to my voice and humble yourself before Him.'

" 'Humble myself before Jesus?' Saul muttered. 'Why would I want to do that? I won't bother His followers anymore, but I'm certainly not going to worship Him. I just want my sight back so I can get on with my life. I don't want to be here, and I certainly don't want you here with me.'

" 'You called Jesus, Lord, when you first fell to the ground,' I continued, undeterred by Saul's words. 'Do you not yet understand that He is the Messiah, the Chosen One of God? It will go much easier for you if you repent of your sin and confess your need for His love and mercy. You might also want to consider my offer of friendship.'

" 'You want me to be friends with you?' Saul asked doubtfully, ignoring my suggestion that he should open his heart to Jesus. 'I don't think so.'

" 'Very well,' I agreed. 'I will sit here quietly until you are ready. Then we can leave.' "

"What happened then?" you interrupt Brokenness, finding her story hard to believe, yet wanting to know more.

"Saul found the chair he had upset when I first greeted him, set it upright, and sat down," Brokenness responded. "The dejection and fear evident in his face must have been close to the pain in his heart, for his lips moved silently from time to time, as though he was praying.

"Suddenly he cried out loud, 'O God, must I leave this place with Brokenness? Is there no other way but this? You, O God, I will forever love. Your Son, I will forever serve. But please, send Brokenness far away from me.'

"I heard my Lord answer him, 'No, Saul, you cannot leave here until you are ready to embrace Brokenness as your friend. I have tried to introduce her to you many times, but you have always avoided her. This time you cannot. When you are ready to accept her companionship, I will tell you what is to happen next.'

"Later Saul reached out his hand as though to touch me. 'Brokenness, are you still there?' he asked.

" 'Yes, Saul. I am here,' I answered him.

" 'Then do something to get me out of this terrible mess,' he pleaded. 'Please, I beg you, do something to help me.'

" 'I cannot help you, Saul, until you choose to help yourself,' I told him.

" 'How can I help myself? I'm blind, remember?'

" 'Oh, I haven't forgotten your physical blindness,' I assured him, 'but I'm more concerned about your spiritual blindness.'

" 'My spiritual blindness?' he exclaimed incredulously. 'Have you forgotten to whom you are talking?'

" 'I know very well who you are,' I assured Saul when he paused to take a breath. 'I should know who you are, since I've followed you many places listening to your self-important arrogance. I have cringed every time you patted yourself on the back, boasting that you are a student of the Law and a Jew from the tribe of Benjamin—as though you had a choice in the matter. Yes, Saul, I know to whom I am talking. For a man who claims to be so religious, you sure have little room for God.'

"For a while Saul sat in silence, as though he was pondering my words. I think he knew that I was right, but he was not about to admit it. 'That's not true,' he defended himself. Then, try as he may, Saul could think of nothing more to say.

"I certainly wasn't going to let that opportunity pass, so I stepped closer and asked him, 'Saul, are you ready to face your mistakes and to take personal responsibility for this so-called mess you are in? Are you truly ready to stop blaming everyone and everything for the problems you have brought on yourself?'

"Saul flinched before he asked, 'Are you suggesting that I am responsible for this situation?'

" 'That's exactly what I'm saying,' I replied. 'I'm not responsible for your misery. Neither is God nor the soldiers who abandoned you here. You alone are accountable for the events that brought you to this time and this place. Had you not closed your ears to the voice of God and insisted on doing

127

what your heart tried to tell you was wrong, you would not be here at all.'

"Evidently my words cut deep into the hardness of Saul's heart, and the excuses he had hidden behind for years provided no escape from my burning probe. 'Forgive me, Lord Jesus,' he sobbed, falling into my arms. 'I have been so wrong. I see my sinfulness and the arrogance of my boasting. Have mercy on me.' "

"That certainly doesn't sound like the Paul I've known," you comment when Brokenness pauses. "I've never thought of Paul as a sinner."

"That's probably true for many people," Brokenness replies. "Contrary to popular belief, Paul was not always the obedient servant who willingly submitted to the will of God. Just like you, he had to learn to live with me.

"At first he was quite unwilling to accept that I should be his friend and companion. Those days we spent together in Damascus after his conversion were important days, days in which we built a foundation of trust and love that never failed us. By the time Ananias laid his hands on Saul, and Saul received his sight and was filled with the Holy Spirit, he was ready to serve the Jesus he had previously persecuted.

"During our days together in Damascus, and later in Arabia, Saul came face-to-face with his inability to please God apart from His grace. That was quite a blow to his ego. He knew that it was hopeless to think that he could serve

God from his own strength. His illusions of greatness had vanished. How Saul cried out to God then!

"When an eagle molts, his feathers come out and the eagle breaks off his talons and his beak. Then he lays on a rock looking like a plucked chicken. Everything that makes him a strong, powerful bird is gone.

"Saul was very much like this in the early years of our relationship. Everything that had given him strength and power had vanished. Although his repentance was sincere, it was not easy for him to leave behind the fantasies that had given him identity and a sense of importance. He was weak and defenseless. Years of self-sufficiency, self-importance, and self-glorification had destroyed his ability to trust and obey God. He struggled as he learned how to depend on God to supply everything he lacked.

"Those early years I spent with Saul were his time of molting, his time of breaking. God sent him into hiding in Arabia so He could change Saul of Tarsus into Paul the apostle. It was difficult at first, but Saul did learn to live with me. Arabia is where Saul and I really got to know each other.

"Saul learned a profound truth there. It is far easier to be plucked and broken in the privacy of your place of prayer and in the company of those who love you and who will pray for you without judgment. When you run from God, you may find yourself being plucked in front of the world, where unloving, judgmental folks brutally mock your nakedness and taunt your weakness without mercy, and certainly without love or compassion.

"Often Saul was overwhelmed by the task God had given him. He just didn't think he had what it took to be God's apostle to the Gentiles. In fact, much of the time he denied that he was even fit to be an apostle. One day he was particularly discouraged.

" 'I'm tired of struggling with this temptation that continually plagues me,' he complained. 'Why doesn't God take it away?'

" 'Perhaps He's using this temptation to keep you from exalting yourself,' I suggested. 'You must admit that pride and self-sufficiency are weaknesses in your soul.'

" 'I know, I know,' Saul hastened to admit, 'but must He continually send me this thorn that gnaws at me, trying to pull me back into the world I vowed to forsake when Jesus entered my life? I get tired of worrying, failing, and sinning yet again. I know I'm not the great person I once thought I was, or the person the world seems to think I surely must be. If they only understood that I am least among the apostles. In fact, I am not even worthy to be called an apostle. Do you realize that I am the greatest, or maybe I should say the worst, sinner there ever was?'

" 'It seems that I am continually having to repent, and repent again. Then I pick myself up and start all over again. Is there to be no end to this litany of sin, repentance, sin, repentance, sin, and repentance yet again?'

" 'What you still don't understand, Saul, is that this sin is not part of you,' I interrupted him. 'Until you stop owning it, you cannot be free to forsake it entirely. It is as though you fear to destroy something that is part of your very self.'

"When Saul did not reply, I thought a moment, then asked him, 'Which of you is stronger? You or God?'

" 'Why, God, of course,' he answered quickly.

" 'Then why are you trying to use your strength instead of His? You are never so strong as when you finally confess your weakness and ask God to do what you cannot do.' "

Turning to you, Brokenness adds, "The molting eagle does not remain a weak bird lying on a rock. Gradually new, thicker feathers replace those that fell out. The eagle's beak and talons grow back with greater strength than before the bird molted. When the eagle yields completely to the process, it soars with greater majesty, greater glory, than it ever experienced before its time on the rock.

"Saul's years in Arabia produced a similar, marvelous change. God did major surgery in his heart as He prepared him to be Paul, the apostle of God to the Gentiles that you have known. His life was changed because his heart was changed. With my help, he saw the truth of who he was and who God had designed him to be. It was then he allowed God to strip him of everything that prevented him from yielding to the destiny God had dreamed for him before he was even born."

Brokenness is silent now. As you ponder this surprising portrait of the apostle Paul, you find yourself comforted by it.

You know that God is changing your heart as you joyfully embrace Brokenness.

Chapter 13

THE PROCESS OF BROKENNESS

I have struggled to save my life,
but I have lost it in the fray.

L IFE WITH BROKENNESS is always full of amazing surprises. She has taught you much, sometimes more than you wanted to learn. At times you have struggled to understand and accept her lifestyle. Her ways, her methods, and her perspective differ vastly from the world system you have always trusted. Many times her counsel seems to be a backward way of looking at things, almost like Jesus' words, "He who seeks to save his life will lose it, but he who loses his life will ultimately save it." Still you have learned to treasure the friendship of Brokenness. She has become your faithful confidante and counselor.

Some days, however, when the struggle to obey is greater than usual, you wish that Brokenness would leave you alone. As she calls your attention to one issue after another, how you wish that she would be quiet for just one day.

"I am tired of all this change," you shout at Brokenness. "I am trying to change. I admit it's not easy, but I am trying. When will I learn to hear the Lord clearly and respond quickly? Just when I think I'm learning, something trips me up and I find myself flat on my face again. And you never relent," you insist, shaking your finger at Brokenness. "How many times must you show me the filth inside myself? How many times must you call me back to repent of the same sin? How many times must I..."

"My friend," Brokenness interrupts softly, laying her hand on your arm, "I don't mean to..."

"Please don't touch me," you say, almost apologizing. "I can't bear your presence today. I just can't."

"I'm sorry that is how you feel," Brokenness replies, the sadness on her face revealing the disappointment in her heart. "If you want me to leave you alone, I will go."

Tears fill your eyes. The absence of Brokenness is not what you want, but you also wonder how you can live another day with her near. "I don't really want you to go," you mumble quietly, "but...but I'm not sure I can live with you, either," you continue, squirming away from her would-be embrace. "If you show me one more hard spot in my heart, touch one more hidden pocket of pain, or reveal one more boarded-up room of resistance, I may not be able to let you stay. I am so overwhelmed, so exhausted. I just can't go on."

"Shall we rest for a while?" Brokenness suggests, leading you to a small cleft in the rock beside the road. "The pathway of change is rarely easy," Brokenness cautions you. "Sometimes in the midst of true revival, old sin habits seem to fall quickly as folks repent and God graciously brings healing and deliverance. More often change requires a steadfast commitment to obey the voice of God. Obedience isn't easy, but it's the only way you can be rid of those sin habits you so despise. Make one right choice after another. God will change what you have been unable to change by yourself.

"In His wonderful mercy and unfailing love for you, He shows you those things you cannot see for yourself. Then He floods your heart with grace so you may endure the change. Trying to alter what you cannot change alone always brings unnecessary pain and serious frustration. Surely you understand by now that changing your heart is not as easy as changing the color of your hair or the style of your clothes."

You nod, acknowledging the truth of her words. Still, you are too weary to go on.

Brokenness smiles her knowing smile. She understands your feelings. "It is quite amazing, isn't it? All these experiences we have struggled through together have brought you to the place where the abiding presence and power of God have become a reality in your life. Sometimes this life of God has welled up in your heart and overflowed freely. These are the days you will remember. They are wonderful and satisfying landmarks in your pilgrimage with Him.

"Most of the time, however, you have had to draw water from the wells of God's salvation deep in your heart. Each time you chose to die to yourself and to submit to the will of

God, you drew fresh water from your heavenly Father's ever-lasting provisions.

"Dying daily is the only way you can tap the Father's power through the presence of His indwelling Spirit. It is like the seed that gives itself to the ground. Now the reservoir for your life is not yourself, but the life of Christ you have allowed Him to plant in your heart. The right choices you have been making have been made possible by His life within.

"The prodigal son learned to make right choices in the hardest way possible. (You know, if you humans would learn how to respond to your Lord's voice, I might be out of a job!) This young man, thinking that he was much wiser than his father, set off on his own to discover wisdom in a very unusual place—a pigpen! To his surprise, that is exactly where he found it. For it was there he discovered the folly of his own way. It was there he realized his selfishness. It was there he recognized that the value and richness of his father's house had precious little to do with money.

"Once he made these discoveries, it did not take long for this lost son to choose to go home. Still his choice to return to his father's house had to be made throughout his journey. Every morning he had to decide afresh to turn toward home and move in that direction.

"Some days as the prodigal and I walked that long road together, he wondered why he had ever started the trip. I encouraged him then, turning his thoughts to what God was trying to change in him. By the time we were within several miles of his home, God had changed much in his heart and he was ready to meet his father.

"Tears of repentance and restoration flowed together that glorious day as father and son embraced and turned together toward home. At first the son struggled to adjust to his new life of obeying his father, but his father loved him, encouraged him, and strengthened him until he became strong.

"The day you repented and promised to obey Jesus as your Lord, you invited Him into your heart. You are God's now, and He is equal to the task of refurbishing you. Simply choose to obey God consciously and continuously, and you too will find that God your Father loves, encourages, and strengthens until you gradually become strong. This is the process of Brokenness."

Chapter 14

THE POWER OF BROKENNESS

I wanted to stand with the mighty, but I found
my home with the broken, the hungry, the poor.

QUIET REIGNS IN THE GRASSY COVE IN THE CLIFFS BESIDE THE BUSY ROAD. YOU ARE NOT NEARLY SO TIRED OR DIS- COURAGED AS WHEN YOU FIRST STOPPED HERE TO REST WITH BRO- KENNESS. In fact, you feel an energy and an interest in life you have not known for quite some time. It is as though you have come into the light after groping your way through dark- ness. And so it is, for the Lord's hand of strength sustains you and His work in your heart gives you the courage to go on.

Brokenness, sensing that you are ready to resume your journey, stands and turns to you. "Are you rested now? Shall we go on?"

"Yes, I'm ready to face life again," you respond.

When you rejoin the others on the road, you find your-self once again leaning heavily on Brokenness. You are certain that her nearness is invaluable to you. Where once you hid your sin, now you repent quickly, willingly, and even joy-fully. You understand the freedom that confession and repen-tance bring.

Truly you are experiencing the benefits of friendship with Brokenness. Her nearness keeps the memory of your failures close to your heart. Yet you do not suffer their reproach. In truth, you are wondrously freed from the con-demning voices that once filled your mind. It is not that the reality or the memory of your sin is gone, for you are still conscious of how and where you have failed. The wonder of your present life with Brokenness is simply that you no longer judge yourself for what is forgiven and in the past. You are free to love and serve your Lord, repenting when you need to, but still loving and serving Him nonetheless.

This same freedom is also changing how you respond to the shortcomings of others. With the memory of your own failures planted firmly in your mind, you find yourself at an amazing vantage point, one you have never before seen and certainly have never before understood. Something beautiful is happening to you. Your attitudes are changing and your judgments seem to be diminishing. Everything is taking on a new perspective.

Brokenness, hand in hand with her Lord, has done a remarkable thing. Gently leading you close to the heart of God your Father, she has forever changed how you look at the world. Now you see and appreciate the hearts of the folks God has put in your life. You understand their struggles and their fears, their dashed dreams and the broken places in their lives. It almost breaks your heart. You never dreamed that they have many of the same joys and sorrows that you do.

Now you know what others are going through. Now you understand what they are up against. Since you struggle with sin that continually plagues you, you rightly conclude that they also experience persistent struggles. Since your hopes are dashed at times, you assume that they too suffer broken dreams and many frustrations.

"Do you understand what's happening to you?" Brokenness asks. "You are beginning to see through the eyes of your Lord instead of through the selfish eyes of a human being. You are being moved by the needs your Father is moved by. You are being constrained to respond based on a heart that loves and wants only to serve the Lord by serving the needs of the people around you."

You nod, admitting the truth of her words. For the first time you are seeing humanity as God sees it—struggling to prosper, struggling for happiness, struggling for fulfillment, struggling for love. You also feel His heartache for these men and women He so carefully created, and hear the groan from much deeper in His heart than you can comprehend. It is as though His heart is broken, and so it is. You see His love for us, a yearning for our well-being so great, so intense, that He gave His Son for our redemption, and you understand that even this ultimate sacrifice did not, cannot, relieve the ache of love deep in His heart. Fellowship and communion, intimacy and oneness, only these will satisfy Him.

Wonder and awe fill your soul as you finally understand that this same overwhelming love, this same driving passion for union that caused the eternal sacrifice of His Son, is just as strong, just as persistent, and just as unrelenting as it has ever been. "Can it truly be," you wonder, "that God will not be content until all of us have come to Him and have given ourselves to His love?" Quickly you turn to Brokenness. Her steady eyes confirm your understanding.

"Not only does God want this union," Brokenness affirms, "but you and all mankind share the need to experience the seemingly elusive yet coveted smile of love and approval from your precious heavenly Father. Your peace of mind, your hopes, and your contentment all hinge on His unconditional love."

The days ahead reveal the importance of this understanding. You really are changing. Your private place of prayer is fast becoming the most exciting room in your life as God's compassion and love release you to pray freely and decisively for everyone who passes through your life. You marvel that an altered perspective can change your life so much.

Then comes the day when Brokenness brings to mind the one person who wronged you so deeply that you swore (literally) you would never forgive him and certainly never pray for him. "Do you remember what happened one very challenging day when...?" You hesitate, wondering if you can avoid the issue—at least for today. One stern look from Brokenness and you quickly begin to intercede for this person as though your future depends on it. (Quite frankly, it does, since only a heart free from the torment of unforgiveness can experience and deliver God's love.)

Brokenness carefully tends the fruit that is planted in your heart the day you finally forgive and pray for your perceived enemy. Tenderly she prunes and prays. She knows that the ripening of this fruit is essential for your future prosperity and well-being. She is certain that you will need to feed on it and draw deeply on its strength if you are to fulfill all that God planned for your life. Each time you yield to God's mercy and love, she smiles her approval.

One day you discover that Brokenness has been planting a new kind of fruit in your heart. How often you have wanted to trust your Lord, taking your hands off His work, but you have not. Indeed, you are only too well aware of how many times you have tried to help God through some of the more difficult situations you and others have faced.

Now, leaning heavily on the wisdom Brokenness has planted in your heart, you find yourself backing off and backing away. In fact, you are embarrassed to even think about forcing your will above God's will for your life and the lives of the folks around you. The mere thought of building your personal kingdom sends you to new depths of repentance and prayer, beseeching Him to prevent such a thing from happening again in your heart. Painfully you allow His purposes to supersede your own, and you put His Kingdom above your kingdom.

Yes, something very real and very grand is happening in your heart. Without effort, you respond to others with greater compassion and more mercy. You find yourself understanding and being patient when others do not live up to your plan for their lives. You even begin to find yourself relinquishing your plan for their lives and turning that very special, very eternal job over to the Lord.

"Thank you," the Lord says when you return His people to Him, allowing Him to be their Lord.

"I'm sorry about that," you mumble. "You see, I didn't understand that…"

"You've no need to explain," the Lord interrupts. "Just don't try to take them back. You can't have them."

Brokenness encourages you through these difficult times of waiting and patience. When you would yield to the temptation to judge another or to be jealous of his good fortune, Brokenness leads you to the place of intercession, far from the chambers of gossip and slander. With the memory of your own struggles and your continual need of mercy and forgiveness planted firmly in your mind, she shows you the sin of your words, thoughts, or attitudes until you are appalled at how easily gossip, slander, and self-righteous anger rule your life. Then you are not quite so quick to be appalled when these faults show up in the lives of other believers.

Not a day passes but that Brokenness faithfully holds a mirror for you to see yourself, lest you become too indignant at the failures of others. Seeing your own face shuts you up every time. "Yes, Lord!" you respond. "Thank You for Your mercy!" Then, with the memory of your failures fresh in your mind, you go back to prayer for the weakness you have detected in another. This time, however, your prayer is bathed in kindness and understanding because Brokenness has caused you to see and understand the work of the cross in your own life.

Now the way you treat people changes dramatically. You are surprised to find that you respond with a compassion, mercy, and love you never thought possible. Repentance fills your heart when you see how wrong you have been and you remember the many times you have been far too quick to judge; far too quick to equate the sin with the person who is sinning; far too quick to banish, shun, and turn the sinner over to satan. You wonder when you decided that it was easier and less painful to disregard the one with sin instead of trying to redeem him.

The power of Brokenness is also evident in the new eyes with which you see the miracle of repentance. You are astonished how wondrously the Lord uses repentance to isolate the corruption of sin, applying His own precious blood to wrap up your iniquity, covering it completely until He can thoroughly remove the damage sin has wrought. How carefully He keeps it under control until loving and non-judging parts of His Body come gently beside you and remove it once and for all from your life.

Yes, true Brokenness is the mercy of God flowing from your heart to other folks who are struggling with sin. It's not that Brokenness seeks to hide the sin, but her nearness prompts you to embrace the one who is struggling, to say, "I know what you are going through; I'm sorry it hurts," and to truly mean it because you have been there, and you maybe still are there. Oh, your sin may not have been made public, but you know that you too could very easily have been caught. You too could be in the place of the person who needs your mercy.

The compassion of Brokenness inspires you to offer mercy in the same way you need mercy. Your heart is softer when she is near. Like no other, she constrains you to encourage others in their battles against sin and to stand alongside them in their moments of failure. Your lips are opened to recount the reality of your own struggles, and your heart empathizes because you have had similar experiences. Even now you know that you struggle with problems that are every bit as serious as the failure facing the one to whom you are called to show mercy.

This is the power behind Jesus' mercy, the power released in true Brokenness. Jesus became human and experienced everything you face so that He could feel with you and for you. Brokenness gives you the same power to share the struggles of others. She teaches you that all men and women are fellow strugglers. Daily she reminds you that mercy cannot be released from a place of lofty pride. Always she is ready to free you from an attitude of superiority or self-promotion. For as Brokenness reminds you who you are apart from Christ, you realize the futility of exalting yourself above another and of promoting yourself and your gifts. You understand that we all have a piece of the truth that we must fit into what others see.

Now you have the courage and the compassion to reach out to God's people. For when she is near, Brokenness draws God's people together and to their knees, fervently praying for one another and for a lost world that desperately needs a people who have discovered her power.

Chapter 15

The Dream of Brokenness

*I have lost what I have gained. I have given
what I was given. I have abandonded my crown
beneath His glory. I am free to serve my Lord.*

"I HAVE A DREAM," BROKENNESS whispers one morning when you join her at your usual meeting place. The mist of the breaking dawn is still pouring off the mountains as the first rays of the sun warm your chilled faces. "It is a grand dream. Would you like to hear it?"

"Oh yes," you eagerly agree.

"I dream of a day when the people of God have completely given themselves to the power of Brokenness. There will be not only one person here and one person there, but a visible company of believers devoted only to our Lord. There will be no imposters, no one wearing masks, no one forcing his own way.

"I dream of a highway there, a highway of holiness where the unclean cannot walk and no lion can prey on His godly ones. I dream of a people who yearn for God's love and who live under the influence of His compassion. This people heals, mends, forgives, and speaks Good News to the poor. They lean heavily on Brokenness, for they are constantly reminded of their need apart from their Lord. They do not forget who they are once they have seen themselves in the mirror Brokenness holds before them.

"I dream of a people who will leap at the sound of His voice, 'Come up hither. Come to the place I have prepared for you, a mansion not in Heaven, but in the Spirit. Come sit at My right hand so that I can teach you of My ways, that you may walk in My path, for from here I will send you to the four corners of the earth, as sowers go out to sow. You will water your seed with the tears of your intercessory prayer as I water the ground with the Holy Spirit. With great joy you will see fruit miraculously arise from the ground.'

"I dream of a people of God who rejoice with great delight as they see His Kingdom grow, even when that growth is through another. They encourage one another, pray for one another, and genuinely share in one another's victories. I dream of a people who know that their times are in the hands of their Lord. They rest with confidence and full assurance knowing that He has laid a plan that they cannot improve upon and that He is directing their future. So they rest in Him, waiting for the sound of His voice and doing with all their heart, without bitterness or regret, whatever is before them to do.

"I dream of a day when the graveyards of this world[1] will no longer hold prisoner the creativity, passion, and tenacity that God gave to humanity to bless the world. No plan God has designed will go uncompleted, no hope will remain unfulfilled, no dream will end before it is finished because this fellowship of saints, composed of ordinary men and women throughout the earth who have abandoned themselves completely to God's plan, will arise with a passion and a commitment to do whatever God requires of them. Their ability, magnified by their union with God through His indwelling Spirit, will surpass anything this world has ever seen, or could ever hope to see.

"I dream of a day when true Brokenness releases the blessings God has planned to be poured on His people in a deluge of supernatural power and glory. In this day, there will be people who are not immobilized by the reality of their humanity. They will have learned that yielding to God, not perfection, is the requirement for destiny. For these folks, holiness becomes the lifestyle of desire, instead of a yoke of legalism."

Brokenness stands now and turns to face you. "I dream of the appearance of these people of God. They will come in all colors, sizes, and shapes, and they will not judge by what they see on the outside. Some will be very young, and others will be very old. They will walk in true unity and love, for the Lord Himself will have melded their hearts together through the power of Brokenness."

---

1. Myles Munroe, *Understanding Your Potential* (Shippensburg, PA Destiny Image Publishers, Inc., 1991), Preface.

Brokenness looks off into the morning sky. "I can see them. They are not far off. These people understand that they will experience this now, in this life. His anointing will flow through them freely—convicting, healing, comforting, reconciling—for they will have long ago given up the right of their own will to embrace His. No personal plans, no individual preferences, will restrict the free flow of the Holy Spirit, for these folks will be completely sold out to God, delighting to obey His every bidding.

"And you, my child," Brokenness whispers again, enfolding you tenderly into her arms, "can be part of this majestic company who will soon subdue the earth with His glory, preferring Him above all others, placing His will above your own, and honoring His dreams even when they would dash yours.

"Self-promotion, personal agendas, and hidden motives have no place here. These vestiges of self-will shut out the very God who calls you. They exclude you from advancing His Kingdom.

"This, my child," Brokenness concludes, "is the Kingdom of which I dream. His Kingdom is advancing, visible in the hearts and lives of men and women like yourself who have chosen to embrace Brokenness and to respond to the gentle nudges of the Holy Spirit deep in their hearts. For wherever soft hearts give the Spirit of God room to live and work, wholeness and joy are the inevitable results.

Thus God's people, those who have made a covenant with Him by sacrifice, cannot help but experience whatever God is doing, longs to do, and most certainly will continue to do. This, my friend, is truly the power of Brokenness."

EPILOGUE

Her home is in the bosom of the Father.
She is the Friend to be preferred above all friends.

BROKENNESS. Since the beginning of human history, she has searched the hearts of men and women to find those who would treasure her wisdom, covet her beauty, and welcome her friendship. There are not many, however, who respond to her voice or embrace her contrary ways, for with her beauty and wisdom comes a rigid and startling responsibility to adopt her lifestyle and imitate her mercy.

Thus many, apprehensive of her tenacious and righteous nature, choose to spurn her, preferring self-determination to surrender, self-will to God's will, and self-dependency to dependency on God. Others simply ignore her, not consciously choosing to reject her, but simply by their busy lives paying her little or no heed. Still others embrace her as the friend she is, the companion who entreats and persists until the last dregs of pride and self-sufficiency are renounced and her place is secure in their hearts.

Haunting and taunting meandering hearts everywhere, Brokenness separates those who die daily from those who seek an easier pathway through their earthly pilgrimage. Where she is, God is. Her home is in the bosom of the Father, the One whose love and mercy gave her birth. Those who embrace her find that life is different, for it is graced with the very presence and power of God. They will see His face in this life, and as they see Him, they become like Him.

Without Brokenness, you will not, and indeed cannot, do what God put you on this planet to do. She waits for you with her hands outstretched, her eyes unyielding. She hopes that you will acknowledge her, trust her, and welcome her as your lifelong companion.

Brokenness—the disdain of tyrants and the wonder of kings. Her mystery has eluded the intellectual and empowered the noble of heart. Can you see in her the very essence of your Lord Jesus Christ? You should, for they are one and the same. They have been forever one, surrendering to the will of the Father and watching to see if you too will give yourself to the will of God, joining the select few who experience the power of the indwelling Christ, who ever has been and now is the power of Brokenness.

RELATED SCRIPTURE REFERENCES

Prelude
Proverbs 11:2
Isaiah 66:2
Matthew 20:25-28
1 John 1:18
Psalm 25:9

Prologue
Psalm 147:3

Chapter 1
Genesis 1-2
Psalm 8
Joshua 24
Genesis 3
Nehemiah 9:31
Psalm 25:14
Jeremiah 8:21-22
Isaiah 57:15-19

Chapter 2
Psalm 86:15
Ephesians 3:14-19
Romans 6:23
1 John 5:16-17
Romans 5:6-8
1 John 4:9-10
Jeremiah 8:22
Psalm 10:17
Job 5:17-18

Chapter 3
Ephesians 2:10
Psalm 1
Psalm 8
Psalm 92:12-15
Genesis 2:24
John 6:63
John 15–16

Romans 8
1 Corinthians 2
2 Corinthians 3:18
Ephesians 1
Genesis 1–2
Psalm 139
1 Corinthians 12
Jeremiah 1:5
Psalm 149:4
1 Corinthians 3:16-17
1 Corinthians 6:19-20
Psalm 132
Isaiah 57:15
Isaiah 66:2

Chapter 4
Genesis 3
John 6:63
Deuteronomy 32:4
Song of Solomon 5:2
Genesis 4:7
Deuteronomy 30
2 Corinthians 3:18
Jeremiah 8:22
Matthew 9:12-13
Hebrews 3

Chapter 5
Isaiah 6
Matthew 7:6
Matthew 26
John 21

Chapter 6
Psalm 141
Ephesians 5–6
John 8:33-44
2 Timothy 2:24-26
Job 5
Proverbs 15:5
Hebrews 12
Isaiah 1
Lamentations 1
Psalm 46:1
Matthew 6:24

Chapter 7
Romans 1–2
2 Corinthians 7:9-10
Psalm 39
Jeremiah 8:22
Hebrews 10
1 John 1:7
2 Samuel 11–12
Psalm 51

Chapter 8
Psalm 103

Chapter 9
John 12:24
Romans 6–8
Ephesians 4:20-24
Philippians 2
1 John 1:9

Exodus 3:14
Psalm 95:8

Chapter 10
Genesis 37,39–45
Psalm 54
Psalm 61
Psalm 23
Matthew 20:25-28
Luke 9:48
Psalm 33:10-11
Proverbs 16:1-3
James 4:10
Matthew 24:45-47
Matthew 25
Romans 8:28
1 Peter 5:5-9
Proverbs 8:13
Proverbs 11:2
Proverbs 16:18-20
Matthew 11:29-30

Chapter 11
Exodus 2–12
Psalm 16:11
Psalm 139
Jeremiah 7:23
Matthew 17:24-27

Chapter 12
2 Corinthians 6:1-10

2 Corinthians 11:22-28
Acts 9
Acts 22:3
Philippians 3:4-6
1 Corinthians 15:9
Ephesians 3:8
1 Timothy 1:15
Romans 7:15,19
Galatians 1:15-17
2 Corinthians 12:1-10

Chapter 13
Luke 9:24
Luke 17:33
Romans 5:1-8
Jeremiah 31:33
Ezekiel 36:26-27
Isaiah 12:3
1 Corinthians 15:31
Luke 15:11-32

Chapter 14
Matthew 6:14-15
Matthew 18:21-35
Mark 11:25-26
John 20:23
John 15
Matthew 5:7
James 2:13
Matthew 5:6
Luke 6:36-38

Chapter 15

Isaiah 35:8-9

Isaiah 11:1-10

Isaiah 61:1-3

Luke 4:18-19

John 14

Luke 8:5-18

Galatians 3:28

Epilogue

2 Corinthians 3:18

1 John 3:2

Other books by
by Don Nori

ROMANCING THE DIVINE
Who among us experiences the fulfillment of divine love? How do we find the One our souls love? Does He love us equally in return? Here is a tale of every person's journey to find the reality of God. It is a tale of hope—a search for eternal love and for all the possibilities we have always imagined would be the conclusion of such a search. In this story you will most assuredly recognize your own search for God, and discover the divine fulfillment that His love brings.
ISBN: 0-7684-2053-9

THE HOPE OF THE NATION THAT PRAYS
The Hope of the Nation That Prays gives clear answers about God's love and His will for America. Will God answer our prayers? What prayers can we pray? What is God's will for America? What is God's will for me personally? Included are prayers for our country and for those we love, based upon scriptures from the Bible. Take a step back in time with prayers from historical figures who have experienced extraordinary answers to prayers in times of crisis. Featured are prayers from such great leaders as George Washington, Martin Luther King, Jr., Abraham Lincoln, and many others.
ISBN 0-7684-3045-3

THE ANGEL AND THE JUDGMENT
Few understand the power of our judgments—or the aftermath of the words we speak in thoughtless, emotional pain. In this powerful story about a preacher and an angel, you'll see how the heavens respond and how the earth is changed by the words we utter in secret.
ISBN 1-56043-154-7

HIS MANIFEST PRESENCE
This is a passionate look at God's desire for a people with whom He can have intimate fellowship. Not simply a book on worship, it faces our triumphs as well as our sorrows in relation to God's plan for a dwelling place that is splendid in holiness and love.
ISBN 0-914903-48-9
Also available in Spanish.
ISBN 1-56043-079-6

SECRETS OF THE MOST HOLY PLACE
Here is a prophetic parable you will read again and again. The winds of God are blowing, drawing you to His Life within the Veil of the Most Holy Place. There you begin to see as you experience a depth of relationship your heart has yearned for. This book is a living, dynamic experience with God!
ISBN 1-56043-076-1

HOW TO FIND GOD'S LOVE
Here is a heartwarming story about three people who tell their stories of tragedy, fear, and disease, and how God showed them His love in a real way.
ISBN 0-914903-28-4
Also available in Spanish.
ISBN 1-56043-024-9

Available at your local Christian bookstore.

For more information and sample chapters, visit www.destinyimage.com

Additional copies of this book and other
book titles from DESTINY IMAGE are
available at your local bookstore.

For a complete list of our titles,
visit us at www.destinyimage.com

Send a request for a catalog to:

Destiny Image® Publishers, Inc.

P.O. Box 310

Shippensburg, PA 17257-0310

*"Speaking to the Purposes of God for This
Generation and for the Generations to Come"*